Still at War

To Sam

Jean Booker

Jean Booker

Scholastic Canada Ltd.

Toronto New York London Auckland Sydney
Mexico City New Delhi Hong Kong Buenos Aires

Scholastic Canada Ltd.
604 King Street West, Toronto, Ontario M5V 1E1, Canada

Scholastic Inc.
557 Broadway, New York, NY 10012, USA

Scholastic Australia Pty Limited
PO Box 579, Gosford, NSW 2250, Australia

Scholastic New Zealand Limited
Private Bag 94407, Botany, Manukau 2163, New Zealand

Scholastic Children's Books
Euston House, 24 Eversholt Street, London NW1 1DB, UK

www.scholastic.ca

Library and Archives Canada Cataloguing in Publication
Booker, Jean
Still at war / Jean Booker.
Issued also in electronic format.
ISBN 978-1-4431-1383-0
I. Title.
PS8553.O64S75 2013   jC813'.54   C2012-906917-5

Cover image of girl © Shutterstock/Gromovataya
Cover image of medal © Shutterstock/Gary Blakeley
Cover image of winter background © istock/Casarsa

6 5 4 3 2 1   Printed in Canada 121   13 14 15 16 17

For Neil, Aileen, Julie, Ryan, Shannon,
Theo and Cal

1

Ellen crossed the school courtyard, pulled open the heavy wooden door and stepped out onto the snow-covered street. Glancing across the road, she noticed a small crowd gathered outside Geordie Cruikshank's bus depot.

What's all this about? she wondered as she ran over to take a closer look. Pushing her way through the cluster of men and women, she saw a man lying on the ground, his leg bent at a strange angle. There was a nasty gash on his forehead and blood all over his face and heavy brown topcoat. One of the German prisoners of war, she realized. She knew Geordie Cruikshank used some of the POWs to shovel the snow off his roof. The man didn't seem to be moving, and three of his fellow prisoners were huddled over him, shouting at each other in German. Suddenly afraid, her first instinct was to turn and run, but she wanted to make sure he was going to be okay.

"Fell off the roof, he did," one of the women in the crowd said. "Hope he's broken his neck."

"Too much to hope for, love," another added. "It's a proper disgrace, them Jerries still being here in England. War's been over for more than a year. Why don't they send the beggars back to Germany, that's what I'd like to know."

"Better still, shoot the lot of them — and anybody else who has owt to do with them."

"Like Geordie Cruikshank, you mean?"

"Aye, him for one."

"Geordie's not a bad sort," a woman in the crowd said. "Besides, the POWs can't be too happy about being stuck here."

Ellen's heart began pounding as a picture flashed into her mind — the German pilot, her dad's old raincoat over his uniform, clambering out of the bombed-out coalhouses in Beeswing Yard.

I've got to stop this, she told herself. I've got to stop thinking about Carl and what happened during the war.

2

"Better be on your way, lass; there could be trouble here," a man standing beside her said. Reluctantly, she turned away and hurried on home up Newgate Street to Beeswing Yard. But as she crossed the cobblestone yard she couldn't get rid of the questions she'd been asking herself for the past two years. What if Carl hadn't made his way back to Germany after she'd helped him escape? It was more than likely he'd been captured, and he could still be here in England. She shuddered to think what might happen to her if anyone found out how she'd helped him. But no one would find out now, would they? It was almost two years since it had happened and nobody, not even her best friend Mavis, knew.

Pushing the fear from her mind, she opened the door with the brass number 2 on it and climbed the stairs to their flat. It was bitterly cold inside, and Ellen noticed the living room window was open a couple of inches at the bottom. She remembered her mam opening it that morning to air the place out after some milk had boiled over on the cooker. She tried to close it, but it wouldn't budge, so she kept her coat on as she lit the fire then started setting the table for tea. Her mam and dad would be home soon.

The fire caught, and when the flat had warmed up a bit she took off her coat and went into her tiny bedroom to get a jumper to put on over her school blouse. The sky outside the narrow window was full of dark, threatening clouds, and her mind flew back to the injured POW. Was he still lying there in the cold? It was awful — all those people just staring, silently hating him, nobody offering to help.

She shivered as she looked down and across the yard to the lavatories and coalhouses that were shared by the five families living in Beeswing Yard. Someone had come and rebuilt the lavs and coalhouses after the bombing. Ellen had heard the toilets and bins had been salvaged from a bombed-out factory in Newcastle.

Just thinking about the bomb brought back the familiar panicky feeling. In her mind, Ellen could still hear the creaking beams, smell the dust and debris surrounding her, smothering her. If the German pilot hadn't come back for her, she knew she would have died. She took a deep breath. Stop it. It's over now; you're safe, she told herself. The war's been over for more than a year. She wondered if these nightmares — although they came as often during the day as they did at night — would ever go away. How she longed to tell someone, to be reassured that she'd done the right thing. But had she?

Her best friend Mavis hated the Germans because her brother, Peter, had come home from the war with only one arm and was shell-shocked. But Carl had nothing to do with that. He was only a boy — not much older than she was. Though she remembered how proud he'd said he was to be fighting for his *Führer*.

Voices from the living room caught Ellen's attention. Her mam and dad must be home. There was a sudden thud and she ran to the front room to see what was the matter.

Her mam was beside the fire warming her hands, and her dad was at the window, trying to force it shut.

"Hello, pet," her mam said. "The window's stuck again. Your dad's trying to keep the cold out."

"Aye, well, it looks as if we'll have to put up with the cold for now," Ellen's dad grumbled. "It's stuck sideways. Darned thing's rotten with woodworm. This flat's fit for neither man nor beast. Something's got to be done about it." He gave up and went to sit in the chair by the fire.

"Why can't we get one of the prefabs?" Ellen asked. The council was building a few houses on the outskirts of Morpeth. They were called prefabs because all the parts were prefabricated — built somewhere else and then shipped and put together. If they got one of those she'd have a big bedroom, and the houses all had running water and inside lavatories.

"They're going to those who need them most. We've been

on the list for almost a year now and still no word." Ellen's mam sighed. "The ones they're building are all spoken for, and I hear they won't be starting any more for another six months, if then."

"I'd better talk to the landlord about the window," Ellen's dad said.

"No you won't. We've nowhere else to go, and there's no sense upsetting him — especially with my job coming to an end and no more work for you after Christmas," Ellen's mam snapped.

"Calm down, lass. It's not my fault all the jobs are going to the blokes who've come back from the war. But I've got that interview with Geordie Cruikshank the morrow. He's looking for a driver. Maybe something'll come of that."

"Let's hope so," her mam said. "Speaking of Geordie, I heard that one of the POWs fell off the roof of his garage today."

"I saw him," Ellen said. "And nobody went to help."

"That's no surprise." Ellen's mam went into the tiny kitchen off the living room and put the chip pan on the stove. Ellen joined her and began peeling the potatoes.

"Can't say as I blame them, do you?" Ellen's dad asked.

"It's not the POWs' fault they're still here," her mam

replied. "I'm sure they'd rather be back in Germany."

"Why *are* they still here?" Ellen asked as she sliced the potatoes for the chips. She'd thought that when the war was over everything would be like it had been before, but it wasn't. There was no ice cream, sweets or fruit in the shops. Food and clothes were still rationed, and there were lots of German prisoners here in England — there were even some living on the farm next door to Mavis's house.

"It's a bit complicated, Ellen. Germany's still a mess, and there are no ships to take them. There's some kind of agreement that we keep so many for a while, and use them as cheap labour to help rebuild things here. And that causes trouble, having them do jobs our own men could be paid to do."

"Did you hear what happened to the POW who fell off Geordie's roof, Mam? Is he okay?"

"Geordie took him to the hospital in one of his buses."

"Geordie's asking for trouble," Ellen's dad said. "Especially if he wants his bus licence renewed in the new year. People are angry enough with him for using the POWs to clear his snow. He should have left the man alone — the other Jerries would have taken care of him."

"But Dad, he was hurt — I saw him. He had a big cut on his head and he wasn't moving." In her mind she could still see the blood splattered like red paint over the man's face, his coat, the white snow.

"I'm not saying it's right, lass, but there's lots who wouldn't mind seeing the Jerries harmed. And Geordie, too, for fraternizing with them. The war might be over but to some the Germans will always be the enemy. Take Mavis's dad. He's always going on about 'rotten Jerries.' I don't know as I blame him — just look at that son of his. What kind of life has he to look forward to with only one arm?"

Ellen's heart started pounding and she had trouble swallowing. Go on, tell them what you did, tell them, tell them, the voice inside her head kept repeating. But just like all the other times she'd tried, the words wouldn't come. The knot of fear tightened in her stomach. She felt sick, and her hands were shaking as she lowered the sliced potatoes into the pan of sizzling fat.

2

The next morning Ellen wakened feeling stiff and cold. As light crept into the room, she pulled the eiderdown over her head and curled her legs up, trying to stop herself from shivering. She felt scared and realized she'd had another nightmare. Bits of the dream came swirling back.

She'd been trying to climb out of a deep hole, hanging on by her fingertips, and then someone had pushed her back in. She remembered sinking, smothering under a mound of snow, someone pushing her down, down . . . then, sheer terror as she saw her own face towering over her. Now what brought that on? she wondered. She recalled the German prisoner who had fallen from Geordie Cruikshank's roof yesterday and realized she was still worried that he might have been seriously hurt. She couldn't imagine how he must feel being ill amongst people who thought he was the enemy.

She pulled her knickers, blouse and gym tunic from the bedside chair in under her covers to warm them. She could hear her mam moving about, lighting the fire in the front room, and then she heard her shout, "Come on, our Ellen, get up. It's snowing again."

"All right, Mam. I'm coming," Ellen yelled back as she got out of bed and struggled into her clothes. She quickly pulled the covers up and straightened them on the bed. As she did so her diary fell to the floor. She'd started writing her daily entry last night but had been too tired to finish it, so she'd just put the journal under her pillow. Now she stooped to pick it up and thrust it under the mattress, where she usually kept it hidden. Carl's name came up more than once. She didn't want it found.

"Hurry up, Ellen! I'm late for work."

"I'm coming, Mam. I'm coming."

Ellen dipped a face cloth into the icy cold water in the wash bowl on her dressing table and dabbed at her face and neck. She ran a comb through her shoulder-length blond hair then went into the front room and stood warming herself in front of the fire.

"Move over, lass," Ellen's dad said as he carried his bowl of porridge over to the brown leather chair beside the fire. "It's going to be cold again today. They say we're in for a doozer of a winter."

Ellen was supposed to try out for the field hockey team at school today, but if it was snowing there wouldn't be any tryouts. There'd been quite a bit of snow already, and it was just December. Usually it snowed only three or four times the whole winter.

"Should I go down the yard and get some more coal for the fire?" Ellen's dad asked.

"No — there's only enough for a couple more days," her mam said.

"I thought Mrs. Lumsden was going to swap us some coal for clothing coupons," Ellen said. Sally Lumsden was a conductress on Geordie Cruikshank's buses and lived down the yard in number 6. Her brother worked down the mines and got coal as part of his wages. He often gave some to Sally.

"So she was, but you need new shoes, and —"

"The hole's not very big. We could stick a rubber sole on it," Ellen said.

"We could, but that'll only last a couple of months and then what?"

"Maybe things'll be better by then," Ellen's dad said.

"Better! That's a laugh! We're worse off now than ever — even the bread's rationed, and it never was during the war. From the looks of things we'll be paying for the war for the rest of our lives. You'd never believe we were the ones who won."

Ellen stared in surprise as her mam burst into tears, flung on her coat and hurried off down the stairs.

"What's the matter with me mam?"

"Oh, it's nowt, lass. She's worried sick about her job at the hospital. And about mine. Which reminds me — I'd better go see Geordie about that job before someone beats me to it." Her dad put his porridge bowl on the kitchen counter and took his shabby brown woollen coat from the cupboard. "Wish I still had that navy raincoat of mine. This old thing doesn't keep out the wet."

Ellen felt her heart beating faster. Her dad was talking about the coat she'd given Carl. The coat the German had forced her to get for him. In her mind she could still see him drawing his finger across Squibs's throat, letting her know what would happen to the rabbit if she didn't help him.

Her mam and dad had had a dreadful row when they'd discovered the coat was missing. Her dad was always losing things, and her mam said he must have left it behind on one of his long-distance driving jobs. Her dad had accused her mam of putting it in with a bundle of clothes she'd given to the O'Briens when they'd been bombed out.

Ellen often wondered what Carl had done with it. If he'd been captured had he been wearing it? She hoped not, because it probably had her dad's name on the lining. During the war her mam had sewn their names on every bit of clothing they owned. Well, almost — Ellen had managed to stop her from labelling her knickers. It had been almost as bad as having to wear those identification bracelets with numbers on them — the ones the government had given them in case they were killed in the Blitz and no one knew who they were. Ellen glanced at the clock. It was time she was off.

"Ta-ta, Dad. Good luck with the job," she called as she put on her green raincoat and ran down the stairs. Outside the snow was falling thick and fast. Should she go to the lav here? She hated using their outside lavatory. Even though she knew the walls had been rebuilt and weren't going to crumble around her, she still felt panicky whenever she had to go there. She decided to wait and use the lav at school. She hurried up the yard and out onto Newgate Street. The school was only a few yards down the street, so she didn't get too wet.

She'd been to the lav and was hanging up her coat in the cloakroom when Mavis dashed in.

"Hockey's cancelled," Mavis said.

"Thought so. The snow's nice, isn't it?"

"Yeah, but look what it's done to my hair. Did you bring the setting lotion?"

Ellen looked at Mavis's long, dark hair. It looked fine to her, but ever since Mavis had got a crush on Bobby Forman she'd been fussing about her hair. Ellen remembered she'd promised to borrow some of her mam's wave set for her.

"Oops, sorry. Mam was so upset this morning — going on about us being so badly off after the war and everything — I clean forgot. I'll bring it tomorrow."

"My dad was on about the war this morning, too. It's those POWs on the farm next door. He'd like to kill every one of them for what they did to our Peter."

"But what happened to Peter — the POWs here in Morpeth didn't do it. I mean, he was shot down in Germany, wasn't he?"

"Hmph. Try telling that to my dad. There's no reasoning with him where the Jerries are concerned. Come on, we're late for class."

All morning Ellen couldn't get her mind off the POWs. Was Mavis's dad right to hate them so much? Ellen was scared of Mr. Ramsbottom, Mavis's dad. He was on the local council and thought he was God Almighty.

Peter had got a medal after the war, and Mr. Ramsbottom had it framed. He forced everybody who went to the house to look at it. Only last week he'd shown it to Ellen and made her try and guess why Peter had been given it. Ellen had said she had no idea, but Mr. Ramsbottom had kept insisting she try and guess. The medal looked like the one her grandfather had been given after the First World War, the one her mam kept in the tin box in her wardrobe. Ellen knew her grandfather had been given the medal for bravery, but she didn't know if that's what Mr. Ramsbottom wanted her to say, and she was afraid of giving the wrong answer, so she'd said nothing. Finally he'd shouted, "Valour, valour, that's what! And what did it get him? Look at him, only one arm and a broken spirit." Ellen had felt her face go red and had mumbled some excuse to get away. But just then Peter had come into the room. He seemed thinner than Ellen remembered him, and she tried not to look at the empty shirt sleeve where his left arm should have been.

"Th-th-that's enough, Dad," he stammered. "Can't you see, she's n-n-not interested."

15

Ellen had quickly made her escape, but even now she shuddered as she remembered the look on Mr. Ramsbottom's face.

By the time school was over there was another inch of snow on the ground. Ellen hurried home up Newgate Street and into their flat. Unlocking the door, she saw a pile of letters on the floor. She leafed through them and saw there was one from Shirley in Canada. They had been writing back and forth for the past year. Shirley was the same age as she was and was a second cousin of her dad's. They wrote to each other almost every week. Ellen ripped open the blue airmail letter. Oh super, Shirley's parents were sending some nylons. They'd already sent two parcels of soap and were always asking if there was anything else Ellen's family needed.

Shirley's older sister, Joan, had been in England with the Canadian Forces during the war. Ellen's dad had lost touch with his cousin and was delighted when he'd met Joan accidentally in London on one of his driving trips. That was how Ellen and Shirley had started writing to each other.

Ellen had just finished reading the letter when her dad arrived home.

"Hello, Dad. Did you get the job?" she asked.

"No, pet, I didn't. Geordie felt Alfie Jones should have it,

16

him being wounded in the war and all. But I've at least one more run with the lorry, and I'm sure something'll turn up."

"Dad, you know Grandad's medal?"

"What about it?"

"What did he get it for?"

"He risked his life to save another soldier. Why?"

"I just wondered if it was like the one Mavis's brother Peter got."

"It's probably much the same, except maybe for the King's head. Your grandfather's has the old King's head on it."

"Can I have a look at it?"

"What?"

"The medal — can I see it?"

"Well, *er*, yes, I suppose you can. Sometime."

"When?"

Her dad had a strange guilty look on his face — the same look Ellen had seen before when he'd done something her mam didn't like.

"What's the matter?" she asked.

"Nowt — and don't go bothering your mam about the medal, or you'll get me in trouble." Ellen waited for him to go on. "I've mislaid the darned thing. I remember taking it out of the box to show Len. It's got to be in the flat somewhere, because I don't think I took it outside. But don't tell your mam. She'd be really upset, and she's got enough on her mind just now."

"Oh, Dad! She's bound to find out."

"Well, it's been a couple of years, and she hasn't found out yet."

"A couple of years! And you think it'll still turn up? Was it worth anything?"

"Maybe, but it's more sentimental value. Don't worry — I know it'll turn up. I'm almost positive I never took it out of the house. Perhaps if your mam's in a good mood when she gets home I'll tell her and we can take another look for it."

But when Ellen's mam came home from work her face was as white as chalk, and she was shaking as she hung up her wet coat.

"What's the matter, Mam?" Ellen asked.

"I've been fired. Not eased out like they said I'd be. I've been told not to bother going back. Can you believe that? We don't have enough money for next month's rent. How on earth are we going to manage?"

3

It snowed off and on for the next couple of days.

"Looks as if we'll be having a white Christmas," Ellen's dad said. "Never happened afore — at least not that I remember. Hope the roads stay clear. I wouldn't want to get stuck in London over the holidays."

It was Saturday afternoon, and Ellen and her dad had just finished listening to a boxing match on the wireless. Her mam was out seeing about a job she'd heard was coming up at Henley's, the newsagent on Bridge Street.

"Christmas Day's not till a week Thursday, Dad. You'll have plenty of time to get to London and back by then."

"Aye, if the load I'm to bring back's ready in time. I want to be home by Christmas Eve to help your mam put up the paper chains. She doesn't like doing it by herself."

Ellen was disappointed that they couldn't have a Christmas tree this year, but her mam and dad had decided they couldn't afford it. The paper chains were always strung across the front room ceiling, and there were lots left from last year.

"Don't forget to let Mam know if you can't get back," Ellen said. The Watersons, who lived above the shop at the top of the yard, had a phone, and Ellen's dad often called them to get a message to Ellen's mam. He was bad about letting them know when he was coming home from long hauls, and Ellen's mam got upset when she was expecting him and he didn't show up. She's been in a bad enough mood since she lost her job, Ellen thought. I don't want her to be upset over Christmas.

She wondered what Christmas would be like this year with no money for presents. They had decided to have homemade ones this time, and Ellen was sewing some handkerchiefs for her dad and an apron for her mam. She hadn't known what to do about a gift for Mavis. Usually they got each other something small. Ellen had been embarrassed to suggest homemade gifts to her friend, but to her surprise Mavis had thought it was a super idea. Now she just had to think about what to do.

"How about a cup of tea, pet?" Ellen's dad said.

"I'll get it. You stay put." Ellen was reaching for the kettle when there was a knock at the door downstairs.

She heard Mavis shout up, "Hello — anybody home?"

"Come in. We're just making tea. Would you like a cup?"

"No, thanks." Mavis bounded up the stairs two steps at a time. "Do you want to come shopping? My mam's given me a couple of bob to spend. Thought I'd get that new Jo Stafford record for Brenda — you know the one — 'Symphony.' I know she really likes it."

Ellen looked at her in dismay. Their friend Brenda was having a Christmas party next Saturday, and they were both invited, along with some other girls from school. But there had been no mention of presents.

"Are we supposed to take presents?" Ellen asked.

"No, I just thought it would be nice to take something. Are you coming or not?"

"Dad, could you get your own tea?"

"Of course, Ellen. You go on. I can look after meself. Oh, you could pick me up the *Chronicle* when you're out — here," he said, counting out the coppers. "There might be a job for me in it."

Ellen put on her green raincoat, tied a scarf over her head and went downstairs with Mavis. They went up the yard, and she wiggled her toes to keep them warm as the wet snow seeped in through the hole in her shoe. The record shop was at the bottom of Newgate Street, and when they got there Ellen was surprised to see some men putting up a Christmas tree beside the old clock tower there.

"Look, Mavis — they're putting up a tree."

"Yes, me dad says there was a big fight on the council about it. He thinks it's a waste of money when some people haven't anything to eat on Christmas Day. The council's not spending anything on decorations though. They're asking everyone who has some to spare to come and put them up on Christmas Eve."

"What a super idea. Let's come and watch, shall we?"

"Okay. Oh! There's Bobby going into the record shop. Come on — let's see what he's buying."

Mavis dashed into the shop, almost slamming the door in Ellen's face. Ellen watched in surprise as she sidled up to Bobby Forman and started talking to him. Reluctantly, Ellen joined them.

"Bobby, we want to ask your advice. Brenda's having a Christmas party, and we're looking for a present for her. What do you think she'd like?"

Ellen stared at her friend in amazement. Mavis already knew Brenda wanted the Jo Stafford record. Why would she say that? Couldn't she see Bobby was embarrassed?

"Well, *er*, there's this new bop record . . ." Bobby mumbled.

Ellen couldn't stay to hear any more. She stood outside the shop waiting for Mavis, hugging her arms across her chest to keep warm, and watched the three men securing the Christmas tree. It looked perfect there beside the clock tower, and Ellen noticed a couple of doves fluttering around it.

The men seemed to be having trouble levelling it, and Ellen heard one of them shout to someone in a nearby truck to bring some tools. She watched as a man in a brown topcoat emerged from the truck. No! It wasn't — it couldn't be. But the POW was young like Carl and about the same height and build. His back was to her as he handed a wrench to the man beside the tree. She just caught a glimpse of his face as he climbed back into the truck, but she was almost sure it was him. Shaking, she ducked back into the record shop and bumped into Mavis who was on her way out clutching a record.

"I bought the bop record. Bobby says it's all the rage, and it'll be great to dance to. Brenda will love it."

What was Mavis going on about? Still thinking about Carl, Ellen just heard the word "dance."

"Dance? Who with? She's not inviting boys, is she?" Could that really have been Carl?

"We can dance with each other. Do you want to come to Woolworths? They've got some of those new bullet brassieres in. You know, like the one Jane Russell wore in *The Outlaw*."

Ellen looked pointedly at Mavis's flat chest. "What for?" she asked.

"Don't be smart. They make you look bigger."

"Bigger — and all pointy. Who'd want to look like that?"

"Well, how about it?"

"Okay, but first I have to get the paper for me dad." Maybe by now the truck with the POWs would be gone. Slinking out of the shop behind Mavis, she was relieved to see that the tree was standing straight and there was no sign of the truck.

They crossed over to Bridge Street to go to the newsagent's shop. It was crowded, and as they went in, Ellen heard voices raised in anger.

"Isn't that your mam?" Mavis asked. Ellen looked over to where the noise was coming from. The shop manager was standing behind the counter, his face red with anger. On this side of the counter, with her back to them, was Ellen's mam, shouting at the top of her voice.

"No, I didn't fight in the war and you know it. What's that got to do with serving behind a counter? What did she do in the war except sit on her fat backside in a government office? I spoke to you before she did and you promised me. You-you —"

Ellen stared in horror. What had got into her mam? People were laughing.

"You give him what for, hinny!" one man shouted.

"She's got a bigger bust, love," someone else said.

Ellen turned and ran from the shop. Slipping and sliding in the snow, she tore home, tears mixed with wet snowflakes running down her cheeks. What was wrong with her mam? How could she do that? In front of Mavis and all those people. She'd never be able to look any of them in the face ever again.

4

As Ellen climbed the stairs to the flat, she heard voices coming from the living room.

"Well, I for one think Geordie needs his head examined. Alfie Jones! Why, the man doesn't know his rear end from his bloody —"

"Watch your language, Len; here's our Ellen. Where's me paper, pet?" Ellen's dad and Len Anderson were sitting at the table. On the patterned linoleum cloth were two mugs with the dregs of tea and an ashtray full of cigarette butts.

"I'm sorry, Dad, I —"

"For crying out loud, you know how important — oh,

never mind, I'll go and get one meself."

Ellen clenched her fists as she went over to the fireplace and jabbed the poker into the dying embers. It wasn't her fault she hadn't got the paper. If her mam hadn't been making all that fuss . . .

"Now, now, don't take it out on the bairn. It's not her fault you didn't get the job."

"I know it, but it makes me blood boil when I think of how Geordie spoke to me — asking if I thought I could work alongside the POWs without losing me temper because he didn't want any trouble. I wouldn't work for him now if he got down on his knees and begged me to."

"Not much fear of that. I told you you were wasting your time asking *him* for a job. But things'll be different in the new year; you mark my words. If the council doesn't renew Geordie's bus licence, that Newcastle firm gets it. I hear they're planning on buying more buses. That'll mean more jobs for the likes of us."

"Will the council really not renew Mr. Cruikshank's licence?" Ellen asked.

"It's possible, lass. Many people aren't happy about Geordie hobnobbing with the POWs — getting them to clear his snow when he could be paying men like us to do it," Len said. "And another thing, it's time Geordie got rid of them conductresses.

It's not right them holding down jobs when there's men with families to support looking for work."

"And why should the women be the ones to go?" Ellen hadn't heard her mam come in, but now she turned and stared at her as she stood in the doorway at the top of the stairs. Len got to his feet, stubbed out his cigarette and reached for a coat that was slung over one of the chairs.

"Don't get your knickers in a knot, love," he said. "I just meant it don't seem right that folks like your better half are looking for a job, when women who have husbands earning good money are kept on."

"And what about those without husbands? Some, like Sally Lumsden, lost their husbands in the war and are struggling to make ends meet. So think before you speak, both of you," Ellen's mam snapped as she took off her coat.

Ellen wished she hadn't asked about Mr. Cruikshank. Now her mam was on her soapbox again. Ellen hated it when she got like that.

"I'd best be off. See you when you get back from London — Wednesday week, if you can make it," Len said to Ellen's dad as he pushed past Ellen's mam and clomped off down the stairs.

"Did you get the job?" Ellen's dad asked her mam.

Ellen held her breath, waiting for a replay of the scene in Henley's shop, but her mam just pulled a face and said, "No, the job's gone to someone with better, *er*, qualifications." Then she burst out laughing.

"What's so funny?" Ellen's dad asked.

"Nowt. Let's have a nice cup of tea, and I'll whip up some mashed tatties to go with the bangers. Come on, Ellen, help me get it ready. What was Len on about seeing you a week Wednesday? That's Christmas Eve, you know."

"Nothing. Just some of the blokes getting together for a pint. Don't worry; I'll be here to help with the decorations."

"There's a smashing big Christmas tree beside the clock tower," Ellen said. "I even saw some doves flying around it. It was lovely. Mavis says everyone's to bring decorations for it on Christmas Eve. Could we make some extra paper chains?" Talking about the tree reminded her about Carl. Had that really been him? She'd barely caught a glimpse of the POW. If it was him, she'd have to be more careful. She couldn't let him see her. If anyone in the town thought she knew him there'd be real trouble. Oh, how she wished the POWs would all go back to Germany and she could forget what she'd done.

"Yes, I think we might manage that. But if this weather keeps up, paper chains won't last long," Ellen's mam replied.

"Now let's get on with the spuds. I'm starving."

Mam's a strange one, Ellen thought as she peeled the potatoes. One minute she's hopping mad, the next she's laughing her head off. It wasn't funny though.

5

When Ellen woke up Monday morning, her father was already up and eating breakfast. "Best get an early start," he said. "It'll take all day to load up, and I've two or three stops on the way down. Have to make sure I'm back Christmas Eve or your mam will be mad at me."

Mention of her mam being mad brought back the dread Ellen had felt all weekend about what Mavis would say when they were back at school.

But when she ran into her before assembly, Mavis seemed to have forgotten all about the scene in Henley's.

"Guess what?" she said as they filed into the gym for

morning prayers. "Brenda's mam says she can invite boys to the party, and guess who's coming?"

"Bobby Forman. Right?"

"Right, and I was wondering if I could stay over at your house that night. My dad doesn't want me going home alone late at night with those POWs being on the farm next to us, and I'd look a right fool if my dad came to get me. Would you ask your mam? Or would you rather stay at our house? My dad wouldn't mind if there were two of us walking home together."

"No, no — I'll ask Mam. Our house is closer to Brenda's." And I don't want to go anywhere near the POWs, Ellen thought. She wasn't looking forward to the party anymore. Why did Brenda have to go and invite boys and spoil everything? If there were boys she'd have to wear something better than her old blue jumper and skirt. She'd asked for a new jumper for Christmas, but that was before her mam lost her job. And what about a present for Brenda? Ellen didn't want to be the only one not taking anything.

Then at lunchtime, when everyone was out in the schoolyard building snow forts and throwing snowballs — things Ellen couldn't remember ever having done before — she got an idea. With all this snow on the ground and more forecast, maybe she could get a job shovelling it. Old Mr. Henderson, who lived at the bottom of Beeswing Yard, might pay her to clear a path to the coalhouses and lavs. As long as Ellen could remember, he'd been an invalid, but he'd been a lot more independent since his daughter, Clara, had married a soldier and gone to live in Newcastle. He still spent most of his time in a wheelchair, though, and certainly couldn't shovel snow. If she earned some money she could get that Jo Stafford record for Brenda. She decided to ask Mr. Henderson that afternoon when she got home from school.

But when Ellen got home she saw that a fairly wide path had already been cleared through the snow. It stretched from the top of the yard at the road down to the iron railings at the bottom where houses number 5 and 6 overlooked the river. Paths to the coalhouses had also been shovelled from both Mr. Henderson's and Sally's houses. Just then Sally came out of number 6 carrying her water bucket. Ellen went to talk to her.

"Hello, Mrs. Lumsden, isn't this snow spiffing?"

"It's spiffing all right. Spiffing nuisance, if you ask me. The buses'll be running late the night, and I'm worn out afore I even start me shift." Ellen noticed Sally had her navy blue conductress uniform on under her mac. She did look tired, and her nose was all red and drippy.

33

"Did you shovel all that snow?" Ellen asked.

"No, hinny. Mr. Henderson's nephew — the one who owns the farm beside the hospital — cleared it," Sally said. "One of them POWs came with him and helped. Nice looking young fella. Just a kid, really. Spoke quite good English. Said he'd learned it here on holiday before the war. Told me he'd been on the run for a while after he was shot down, but was caught in Newcastle and sent here to work on the farm. They're in Mr. Henderson's house now having a cup of tea to warm them up. It's good to see the prisoners doing something to earn their keep."

One of the POWs right here in Beeswing Yard! What if it was Carl? Hadn't he told her he'd learned some English when he was here on holidays?

A blast of cold wind swirled up the yard, and Ellen shivered. She glanced at the snow that had drifted up outside number 3, where Joe and Sylvia Barker lived. Joe Barker was a foreman at the Ashington coal mine, and if he was on the late shift his wife would have to shovel the snow when she got home from her job.

"Do you think anyone else would like their path cleared?" Ellen asked.

"Well now, Nellie Diamond would probably be glad of a hand, and I'm sure your own mam and dad wouldn't say no to some help." Sally turned off the tap and bent to lift the bucket of water.

"But I couldn't charge them," Ellen said.

"Charge? Oh, I see — trying to make some extra pocket money for Christmas, are we?"

"My friend Brenda's having a party, and I haven't any money for a present."

"Well, you'll get nowt from that stuck-up lot in number 3, and the rest of us are struggling as it is to make ends meet. But I've got a spare bottle of Evening in Paris scent. You're welcome to it if you think your friend would like it."

"That would be super, Mrs. Lumsden. Are you sure?"

"Yes, I'll go and look for it."

"Oh, thank you! I'll wait out here for you," Ellen said.

She watched Sally head back to number 6 with her bucket of water. The scent wouldn't be as good as the Jo Stafford record, but it was better than nothing, and it was kind of Sally to offer.

Ellen plodded through the snow to the iron railing overlooking the gardens that belonged to Sally and Mr. Henderson. Beyond them, the River Wansbeck was a solid sheet of ice.

Every time Ellen looked through these railings she thought about Carl jumping over them. He'd managed to escape from Mavis's dad and the Home Guard by running to the river and taking Sally's old boat. Ellen had been so scared there'd be a ruckus about the boat going missing, but when Sally complained everyone in the yard had just shrugged and said it was no surprise to them. Sally, who was known as Sloppy Sally to her neighbours, was careless with her things, so everyone assumed she mustn't have tied it up properly and it had just drifted off.

Someone had found it a couple of days later, wedged between two of the stepping stones further downstream, and returned it. Now it lay in the middle of Sally's garden, all covered with snow like a shrouded coffin.

Ellen was frozen and wished Sally would hurry up. Perhaps she should offer to help her find the perfume. She turned away from the railing and made her way to Sally's door — just as two men came out of Mr. Henderson's house.

Horrified, Ellen realized one of the men was Carl. She quickly turned her back to them, but as Carl walked by her he whispered, "We must talk — meet me at the clock tower at four tomorrow, *ja*?" Before she could say anything, he was gone up the yard and out onto the street.

What did he mean they "must talk"? Didn't he realize the danger he was putting her in? There was no way she was going to meet him — ever. If anyone saw her with him, dear knows what would happen to her. She'd lose all her friends, and her mam and dad might disown her. And what would Mavis's dad do? She should never have helped Carl escape. She should have known he couldn't get back to Germany. Now what was she going to do?

Just then, Sally came hurrying out of her house. She was carrying a small dark blue bottle. "Here we are. I — whoops!"

Ellen watched in shock as Sally slipped on the icy pathway, tried to regain her balance, then fell, hitting her arm on the cement step. The bottle of scent went flying through the air into the snow.

"Are you all right?" Ellen rushed to help her. Sally took Ellen's arm and tried to get up, but she winced in pain and gasped, "Eeh, lass, I can't seem to get me breath."

"Stay still. I'll be right back," Ellen said. Then she ran, slipping and sliding, up the yard to fetch her mam.

6

Ellen tore up the stairs to the flat two at a time.

"Mam, Mam! It's Sally — Mrs. Lumsden — she's hurt."

"What's the matter? What's happened?" Ellen's mam appeared at the top of the stairs, a skein of white knitting wool in her hands.

"Sally — she's slipped and hurt herself. She can't get up," Ellen said.

"I'll be right there." Ellen's mam dropped the wool and grabbed her coat from the hook on the wall, struggling into it as she hurried down the stairs.

"She can't use her arm. She says it hurts to breathe," Ellen said as she followed her mam down the yard to where Sally lay sprawled across the stone step.

"I'm all right. There's nothing broken. I just need — oh dear, I've come over all funny. I —" Sally was as white as a ghost.

"Hush. We'll have you inside in no time. Here, Ellen — you take one arm, and I'll take the other. Now, lift, but be careful."

They managed to get Sally into the house and onto her bed.

"Put the kettle on and make some tea, pet. I'll check her over and make sure there's no bones broken," Ellen's mam ordered.

Ellen found the tea and a pint pot amongst the dishes piled in the kitchen sink. The living room was littered with magazines, cups half full of old tea and ashtrays overflowing with cigarette butts. Chairs were strewn with clothes. Ellen finally found the sugar bowl under Sally's conductress cap on the kitchen counter.

The living room window looked out onto the garden and the river. The kitchen was small but had lots of cupboards. As she took the tea into the bedroom, Ellen glimpsed another bedroom. Its window also looked out over the garden. It's much nicer than our flat, Ellen thought.

"Would you like Ellen to go for Dr. Davidson?" Ellen's mam asked.

"No, no, hinny. I've never been to a doctor in me life, and

I'm not starting now. It's just a few bruises. I'll be all right in a minute. Anyway, I've got to get to work. Oh, my goodness, look at the time! I've still got to have my supper. If I don't get a move on I'll be late." Sally tried to get off the bed, but when she put weight on her wrist she fell back with a cry of pain.

"You can't go to work like this," Ellen's mam said.

"I have to. There's no one else, and with all this snow . . . Unless — would you fill in for me? Just for tonight. I'm on the five to eleven shift."

"Me?" said Ellen's mam in surprise.

"Yes, you. We're about the same size. My uniform would fit you nicely. It's easy. You just take the money and punch out the tickets."

"Oh, no, I couldn't. I —"

"Please. If I don't show up Geordie'll give me the sack. There's not time now for him to get somebody else. Besides, if you do a good job he might take you on permanent-like. Mary Fogerty's thinking about going to live with her cousin in Newcastle. Her mother caught her fraternizing with one of the POWs and threw her out of the house. She's staying with a friend, but it's only temporary, so Geordie will be looking for someone else."

Ellen's hand shook as she handed Sally the tea. Would *her* mother throw her out of the house if she knew what she'd done? Would she understand why she'd helped Carl, or would she be upset and angry?

"Thanks, love," Sally said. "Ah, that tastes good."

Sally took another sip and looked up at Ellen's mam. "Well, what's it to be? Yes or no? You'll have to make up your mind, 'cause if it's no it'll take me a while to get meself ready and off."

"You can't go to work like this," Ellen's mam said.

"That's settled then."

"But *you* need help."

"Ellen can look out for me, and you'll be home shortly after eleven. Now help me out of this uniform. Ellen, you go and round up my cap for your mam, it's in the kitchen, and there's a black leather money bag somewhere near the laundry basket. And don't forget your scent. The bottle landed somewhere in the snow when I went down. Let's hope it's not broken."

Outside Ellen found the bottle of Evening in Paris lying intact on the snow. The silver label was a bit wet. Ellen wiped it on her coat, hoping it wouldn't look smudged when it dried out. Back in Sally's house she got the cap and found the money bag under a heap of dirty laundry.

"Well, what do you think?" Ellen's mam said as she emerged from the bedroom wearing Sally's uniform.

41

"Hmm, not bad. The skirt's a bit tight round the backside though, isn't it?" Ellen teased.

"No, it isn't," her mam snapped. "Here, give me that hat." She plonked it on her head and glared at herself in the mirror over the mantelpiece.

"What are you gawking at? Do I look that bad?" she demanded.

She's touchy today, Ellen thought. Better change the subject.

"No, you look smashing, Mam," Ellen said. "By the way, I was wondering if Mavis could sleep over at our house after Brenda's party on Saturday."

"What for? What's wrong with her own house?"

"Nothing, but she doesn't want her dad to fetch her, and he says she's not to go home by herself because of the POWs on the farm next door."

"Yes, she can stay. Her dad's being ridiculous, though. The prisoners wouldn't hurt her."

"Mavis says he's like that because of what the Germans did to Peter. He sits for hours, just staring out of the window."

"Poor Peter. I can understand how Mr. Ramsbottom feels, but sometimes he goes too far. Sally's just told me he's been trying to get the other councillors to vote against renewing Geordie's licence at the meeting next week. It's only because he gets the POWs to help around the bus depot."

"Do *you* think it's okay for Geordie to use the POWs?" Ellen asked.

"I don't know if it's okay, but I do know that Geordie has the right to use who he wants. And if he chooses to hire the POWs and there's some who don't like it, that's their problem. They don't get paid much. Just pocket money, really. Same for the work they do on the farms. He doesn't give them the better paying jobs."

"Len Anderson doesn't like it. He doesn't even like Geordie having conductresses on the buses. I wonder what he'd say if he knew you were going to be one of them."

"I don't care what Len thinks. We need the money and that's all there is to it. If Geordie'll pay me, I'll work for him."

"What about me dad?"

"What about him?"

"Geordie didn't hire *him*. Dad said he wouldn't work for him now if he begged him to. He won't like *you* working for him."

"Your dad didn't tell me that. He just said the job had gone to Alfie Jones. It's probably because your dad is friends with Len that Geordie didn't take him on. Geordie knows how Len and his pals feel about the POWs. Well, what your dad doesn't know won't hurt him. I'm only filling in for tonight. If I get more work we'll just have to deal with it then."

The mention of more work made Ellen wonder if a new jumper might be a possibility after all. She took a deep breath. "Mam, do you think — could I — you know that jumper I asked for for Christmas? Would you — could I — have it a bit early? So that I could wear it to Brenda's party?"

Her mam frowned. "There'll be no jumper now, pet. Not with your dad and me out of work. Besides, I thought we'd agreed just to have homemade gifts this year."

"Maybe you could knit me one?" Her mam was good at pulling out old jumpers and using the wool for new ones.

"Not before next Saturday I couldn't. I have to get going. You stay with Sally till I get back. She says there's kippers and black pudding in the pantry and potatoes under the kitchen sink. There'll be enough for both of you. Ta-ta, pet." She patted Ellen's arm as she hurried out the door.

Disappointed, Ellen set to work washing the pile of dishes in the sink. Her mam was good at knitting, and she *was* knitting something. Ellen remembered seeing the white wool her mam had been winding when she'd fetched her to help Sally. Maybe the white wool was for socks or mitts or something practical like that — but white wasn't very practical for mitts, was it?

Sally fell asleep after her supper, and Ellen huddled close to the fire to keep warm. Outside the wind howled, and a cold draft blew in under the front door. She threw some more coal on the fire, then put her coat on and sat closer to the flames. She was almost asleep by the time her mam came home at a quarter to twelve.

"How did it go?" Ellen asked.

"Well, the job's not all it's cracked up to be, and the drunks on the last bus were something else. But I must have done all right, 'cause Geordie says if Sally's not up to it tomorrow I can fill in again. How's she been?"

"Not too good. She ate dinner, but she said her chest was very sore. She fell asleep after that."

"Oh dear, maybe we should have got the doctor. She might have cracked her ribs. I'll have to see how she is in the morning. You run along home now, and I'll make sure she's settled for the night."

Outside, the snow had swirled into soft drifts. The paths that had been cleared earlier had almost disappeared, and Ellen found it hard going to get across the yard and up to number 2. She couldn't get Carl out of her mind. What was so important that he had to talk to her? She was curious, but she knew that she couldn't take the risk of meeting him.

7

For the next few days Ellen panicked every time she caught a glimpse of a POW, but there was no sign of Carl. She made certain to stay well away from the clock tower.

"What's the matter with you?" Mavis asked as they left the schoolyard on Friday afternoon. "You're so quiet. Are you still worrying about what to wear to Brenda's party tomorrow? If you like you can borrow one of my jumpers."

"No, it's all right. But thanks. I'm just not in the party mood." Ellen's mam had said she could borrow her very best crystal beads to wear. When Ellen had tried them on with her old blue jumper, she'd decided it didn't look too bad after all.

As it turned out, it didn't matter what she wore. She spent most of the party bundled up in a hat and coat, skating and sliding with her friends. Brenda's dad had surprised them with two old pairs of skates he'd found, and everyone had gone to the River Wansbeck. None of them had ever skated before — they'd never even seen the river frozen over until this winter.

The skates were a bit big, and the blades were rusty, but everyone was eager to have a turn trying them out. At first Ellen was afraid she'd fall, but after a few minutes she relaxed and began to enjoy the feeling of the wind against her face and the sound of the blades cutting into the ice.

"Hey, not bad. Where'd you learn to skate?" Ellen turned around to see Bobby coming toward her — until he hit a bump in the ice and fell. He slid into her, knocking her down beside him. Embarrassed, she tried to scramble to her feet, but she slipped and fell again, this time landing right on top of him.

"Hey, she's fallen for you, Bobby," someone shouted. Ellen heard everyone laughing as she finally managed to get to her feet and stagger over to the snow bank at the edge of the river. Her skirt and stockings were soaked through.

The gang soon returned to Brenda's house, and Ellen took

off her wet skirt and stockings so Brenda's mam could hang them in front of the fire in the kitchen to dry. Brenda loaned her one of her skirts. They'd all brought slippers to change into, so Ellen's feet were warm enough, but her legs were freezing.

After sandwiches and lemonade, Brenda's parents stayed in the kitchen and left them alone in the front room. They played charades for a while, and then Brenda put on the Jo Stafford record that someone had brought to the party. Several people started dancing, and Ellen felt uncomfortable and out of place.

Then, to her surprise, Bobby came over to talk to her. "Sorry about bumping into you on the ice," he said.

"That's okay," Ellen replied. Then he just stood there looking awkward, as if he didn't know what to say or do next. Desperately, Ellen tried to think of something to say.

"Have you seen the Christmas tree beside the clock tower?" she blurted out.

"Aye — and there's doves there making a nest."

"In a Christmas tree?"

"Aye. Want to dance?" he asked abruptly.

And Ellen, not wanting to be rude, nodded yes.

He wasn't much of a dancer and kept stepping on Ellen's

toes. She could see Mavis scowling at them from across the room. All of a sudden she felt something snap around her waist, and then her knickers started to slide down over her hips. The elastic must have broken when she fell!

She'd mentioned to her mam last week that the elastic in her knickers was getting slack, but there was no elastic in the shops, so her mam had pulled it through and sewn it tighter. The stitches must have given way.

"Oh, no!" she gasped and left Bobby standing open-mouthed as she fled, red-faced, clutching her hips, upstairs to Brenda's bedroom. Yanking up the skirt, she snatched the sliding knickers and made a grab for the end of the elastic — just in time to see it slither into the waistband.

Desperately she searched Brenda's dressing table for something — anything — she could use to fish it out. Nothing. Not even a safety pin. Then she noticed a large bottle of Evening in Paris sitting on the silver tray and realized Brenda already had some of the scent she'd brought. What must Brenda think of her measly little bottle?

Suddenly it was all just too much. She couldn't go back downstairs, she just couldn't. She let the knickers fall to the floor and plonked herself down at the dressing table. She stared into the mirror, watching the tears ooze from her eyes and trickle down her face. Just then there was a rap on the bedroom door. Ellen heard a giggle as Mavis came hurrying in.

"Come on, Ellen. We're going to play postman's knock. What's the matter? Why are you crying?"

"I'm going home."

"But why? You can't go home — I'm staying at your house, remember?"

"You'll just have to get there on your own!" Angrily, Ellen stamped down the stairs and walked through the living room. She pushed past the dancing couples and went into the kitchen where Brenda's parents were listening to the wireless.

"Your things are dry, Ellen," Brenda's mam said. "Here, just nip into the pantry and put them on. Are you enjoying the party?"

"Yes, thank you, Mrs. Hind, but I have to go now." Ellen took the stockings and skirt from her and ran into the pantry, hoping Brenda's parents hadn't noticed her tear-stained face. Somehow Ellen managed to get her coat and sneak out without anyone noticing. She was so upset she didn't wait for Mavis, who was struggling into her coat as Ellen stormed by. She was halfway up Newgate Street when Mavis caught up with her.

"Hey, wait for me. What's the matter with you? Why'd you run off like that? We should have stayed. I think Bobby was going to ask me for a date."

"Hmph," Ellen grunted.

"He's so nice," Mavis went on. "Imagine him asking you to dance."

"What do you mean?"

"Well, he obviously saw you sitting all by yourself. It was so nice of him to ask you, don't you think?"

"Bobby's a drip!" Ellen snapped. Was Mavis suggesting that Bobby had only asked her out of pity?

"No, he's not! And you'll never get a boyfriend if you keep running away from them."

"I don't want a boyfriend," Ellen snapped again. Was that true? She wasn't sure. Maybe. But she didn't want to play silly kissing games like postman's knock. Yet, she couldn't help wondering what it would be like to kiss a boy.

Mavis babbled on about Bobby all the way up Newgate Street.

"You know what he told me — but he made me promise not to tell anyone, so you mustn't mention it to a soul. He said that last night, when he was checking on the doves, he overheard Len Anderson and some of the men outside the

Black Bull pub plotting to do something to Geordie's buses."

"What do you mean?" Ellen asked as they turned into Beeswing Yard.

"You know — smash them up or something."

"They wouldn't do that! He was having you on."

"No, he wasn't. They said they were going to teach Geordie a lesson for getting POWs to work for him."

They had to be quiet when they went into the flat because Ellen's mam was asleep. But all the time they were getting undressed, Ellen wondered if what Mavis had told her was true. If it was, should she tell her mam? It would be awful if someone did something to the bus her mam was working on. Mavis had said not to tell anyone, but *she* hadn't promised, had she?

It wasn't till after they were in bed, snuggled under the covers and trying to keep warm, that Ellen remembered she'd left her knickers lying on the floor in Brenda's bedroom.

8

Ellen wakened to find Mavis still sleeping, curled up in bed beside her. A gust of wind shook the bedroom window, and Ellen huddled back under the eiderdown. What's keeping me mam this morning? Ellen wondered. Usually her mam was up before anyone else, starting the fire, even on Sundays. Ellen decided to get up and light the fire so it would be warm for her mam and Mavis when they got up.

She slipped out of bed, shivering as she put on her red woollen dressing gown and leather slippers, and tiptoed over to the door to her parents' room. Even with her slippers on, the linoleum felt cold. As she pushed open the door there was a strange sour smell. She heard the sound of vomiting, and there was her mam, leaning against the side of the bed being sick into the chamber pot.

"Mam! What's the matter?" Ellen asked, running over to her.

"It's all right, pet. It's nothing. I didn't have time to go down to the lav." Her mam straightened up and wiped her mouth. "The sausage I ate last night must have been off. You go and light the fire. It's freezing in here. I'll be there in a jiffy."

I hope Mam stops being sick before Mavis gets up, Ellen thought. She put a match to the newspaper and kindling in the grate, then tipped the coal from the scuttle on top of them.

Mavis had an inside lav in her house, and her chamber pots were just for emergencies. In all the times Ellen had been at Mavis's house she'd never seen one with anything in it. She'd just die if Mavis saw her mam throwing up.

She needn't have worried. By the time Mavis appeared in the front room, rubbing the sleep from her eyes, Ellen's mam was feeling better and had been down the yard to empty the chamber pot.

"Eeh, it is cold," Mavis said, warming herself at the fire. "You had me awake half the night, Ellen — tossing, turning and talking in your sleep."

Ellen froze. What had she said?

"She's done that ever since she was trapped in the lavs after the bomb fell," Ellen's mam said. "Here, let me put some more coal on the fire. It's not half as cold in here as it is outside. I think the water pipe in the yard's frozen. I had a devil of a time turning the tap on, and all I got was a measly dribble. How was the party?"

"Spiffing!" "Not bad," Mavis and Ellen said at the same time.

Ellen's mam laughed. "Are you sure you were at the same party?" she asked. She seemed a bit better, and Ellen noticed the colour had come back into her face. But when they sat down to breakfast, she only drank her tea and didn't eat any of the fried bread.

"Tell me about it then," Ellen's mam said. "Who was there? I met Brenda's mam in the chemist's, and she said you would be skating. I've always wanted to try it, but it's only the second time I remember the river freezing, and I think I'm a bit past it now. What was it like?"

"It was okay, once I got the hang of it and stopped falling," Ellen said.

"The boys were better than we were," Mavis said. "Especially Bobby Forman."

"Oh, there were boys there then. What else did you do besides skating?"

"We danced," Mavis replied. "Bobby taught me how to bebop. He's a super dancer."

Ellen swallowed her tea the wrong way and almost choked. Bobby only had two steps: one forward and one back — and in between he'd done a funny little wiggle with his bum. He certainly was no Fred Astaire.

"What was wrong with the party, Ellen?" her mam asked.

"Nothing. It was all right. I don't like dancing, that's all. Mam, could we get the paper chains out today?" Ellen didn't want to talk about the party.

"Yes, after we've done the dishes, if you like. Are you staying, Mavis?"

"I'd love to, but my mam's stippling my bedroom today, and she said I have to help. We're doing it pink and green. Brenda's mam did her room and it looks smashing."

She's so lucky, Ellen thought. I wish Mam would do my room. I hate that old brown-and-orange-flowered wallpaper. It had been on forever and was all watermarked where the window had leaked. There wasn't any real wallpaper to be had in the shops, but stippling was all the rage. Mrs. Waterson had done one wall of her shop using a cut potato dipped in paint to make the pattern, and it looked super.

"I'd better get going," Mavis said.

Ellen went to the bottom of the stairs with her and was reaching for the latch to open the door to the yard when Mavis suddenly said, "Who's Carl?"

Ellen gulped. She could feel her heart hammering in her chest. "Wh-what are you talking about?" she stammered.

"Carl. Who is Carl? You were talking about him in your sleep."

Oh, no! I didn't. I couldn't have, Ellen thought in panic.

"I-I don't know what you mean. I don't know anybody called Carl."

"Come on, you can tell me. We are best friends, aren't we?"

Mavis couldn't find out about Carl. She just couldn't. She might let something slip to her dad, and then what?

"You must have heard wrong. I told you — I don't know anybody called Carl."

"No, I didn't! Plain as day it was. 'Carl.' You were thrashing around and said it more than once."

"Close the door, girls. You're letting in the cold," Ellen's mam yelled from upstairs.

"I'll be off then. See you tomorrow." Mavis gave her a speculative look as she stepped outside.

She doesn't believe me, Ellen thought as she climbed back

upstairs. And she won't let it drop; I know she won't.

"You still having nightmares then, pet?" her mam asked when she was back in the living room.

"It's the first in a long time," Ellen lied. "It was nothing. Where are the decorations?"

"In the sideboard drawer. Listen, I know you don't want to talk about the time the bomb dropped, but if it's still bothering you it might help."

Oh, how I would love to talk; to tell you and Dad all about it, Ellen thought. But she knew she couldn't tell anybody. The only place she could "talk" about it was in her diary, and even then she had to be careful. She felt tears coming and quickly went over to the sideboard and yanked the drawer open.

"I'm fine, Mam. Really I am. Shall we start with the red or the green?"

"The green. I hope your dad gets back in time to help put them up."

"He said he would. Though I think he said he'd see Len on Christmas Eve, too."

"You're right, and I wish he wouldn't. That Len's nothing but trouble."

"What do you mean?"

"He's up to no good. I heard he's been bad-mouthing Geordie."

Should I tell her what Bobby told Mavis about someone damaging the buses? Ellen wondered. But she decided it might be best to wait until her dad got home and ask him about it.

"There are doves in the Christmas tree beside the clock tower," Ellen said, changing the subject. "Bobby says they're making a nest there."

"A nest? This time of year? Doves usually nest in February or March. They must be daft if they're building one in a Christmas tree."

"Maybe they don't know it's not a real tree growing there."

"Obviously, they don't. On the other hand, could be they're like us, desperate for a decent place to call home and willing to settle for anything."

"Oh, Mam, we're not desperate."

"Not yet, but when Sally's better I could be out of work again. Even with my wages we're still a couple of weeks behind with the rent. If your dad doesn't find something soon, I'll have to pay a visit to the pawn shop."

"You wouldn't!" Ellen would just die if any of her friends saw her mam going into the pawn shop.

"Why not? I'm not too proud to go there. I could get a few quid for my wedding ring."

"Mam, not your wedding ring!"

"No, lass," her mam laughed. "I wouldn't part with that. There's that old silver tea set of my mother's, or maybe that old gold watch of your grandfather's — it's just sitting in a box in the cupboard. Or that medal of his, maybe that's worth something." She turned toward the bedroom, as if to look for it.

Oh no! Ellen thought. Not the medal. What if she discovered it was missing? She had to get her mam's mind off it.

"Mam, I have to tell you something. Mavis said Bobby heard some men outside the pub threatening to teach Geordie a lesson. They're thinking of doing something to the buses."

"Oh dear, there's going to be trouble. I know there is. I only hope your dad's not mixed up in it."

"Dad wouldn't do anything like that — especially with you working on the buses."

"Maybe not, but I wouldn't put it past Len. Besides, your dad doesn't know I'm working for Geordie. He left before Sally had her fall, remember? Don't you worry about it, but thanks for telling me. If there is going to be trouble it's better to be ready for it than be taken by surprise. Now let's get on with these paper chains and forget about everything except Christmas."

9

The paper chains were all ready and waiting Christmas Eve, but by four o'clock Ellen's dad still hadn't arrived home from London. He had phoned the Watersons's shop on Monday afternoon to say he was running a bit late because of the bad weather and because he'd had to stop off on the way back to pick up more stuff. But he was sure he'd make it home early Wednesday.

"What's keeping him?" Ellen asked for the umpteenth time. "They'll be starting the tree soon."

"It's probably the weather. They've had dreadful storms down south, and I hear some of the roads are blocked. Why don't you go ahead, and if your dad gets back before I have to go to work we'll both come on down. I'll leave him a note if he's not home when I go. But mind, if neither of us makes it, be sure to come straight home when the tree's finished."

"But what about our own decorations? You won't be home till nearly midnight." It was bad enough they couldn't have a tree this year, but it would be awful without the red and green paper chains hanging from the ceiling.

"That's the least of my worries right now. My shift's not going to be easy tonight. Everyone'll have finished work early and been into the pubs and . . ."

"Does Dad know about your job?" Ellen asked.

"No — thought I'd wait till he gets home."

"If you're at work when he gets home, what'll I say?"

"Better tell him. I was hoping to break it to him gently, but it doesn't matter. Anyway, off you go, or you'll miss it."

Ellen slipped her coat on and hurried down Newgate Street. It was getting dark, and most of the windows in the houses along the street were lit. Ellen glanced into some of them as she passed. When the war was on, the windows had all been blacked out. Now it was nice to be able to see inside and get a glimpse of other people's lives.

As she neared the clock tower, snow began to gently fall on

the crowd gathered there. She pushed through and put the paper chains into the large box beside the Christmas tree. It was filled with an assortment of shiny coloured balls, paper snowflakes, streamers and ornaments of all shapes and sizes. A tall ladder stood beside the tree, and Fred Boggs, the butcher, was handing the decorations up to Mayor Shuttlewood, who was precariously balanced halfway up.

"Further up — put it further up," a man in the crowd shouted.

"No, no, not there, you stupid old fart! Now it's cockeyed!" a woman yelled. There was laughter all around as the mayor reached out to straighten the glass ball, swore and almost lost his balance.

Ellen looked around for Mavis but couldn't see her anywhere. Where has she got to? she wondered. I was sure she'd be here ahead of me. Ellen wandered around the edge of the crowd looking for her and had just decided to give up when she felt a tap on her shoulder from behind.

"There you are. Oh!" she gasped as she spun around and found herself staring at a POW. Her gaze moved from the brown topcoat to the familiar face. Oh, no — not Carl!

"Go away. Leave me alone," she hissed as she turned away from him.

"*Fräulein* Ellen — *please*! Something I have, I must give to you."

"Hello, Ellen, where've you been?" Ellen looked around to find Mavis coming toward her. Thank goodness Carl was moving away. Had Mavis seen him? She must have. Had she heard him say her name?

"What did that POW want? What did he say to you?" Mavis asked.

"Noth-nothing. He was asking about the tree. That's all," Ellen stammered, hoping Mavis wouldn't ask what it was he'd wanted to know. She hadn't the foggiest idea what she'd say.

She was relieved to see that Carl had completely disappeared into the crowd. She breathed a silent prayer of thanks when Mavis pulled a face and said, "What a nerve!"

Then she asked Ellen if she'd seen Bobby. "I've looked all over for him. He said he was coming."

"He must have changed his mind." Ellen was still shaken from seeing Carl. She needed some time to think about what had happened. What had he said? Something about giving her something? What on earth could he mean?

They stayed and watched until the tree was completely decorated. There was lots of cheering and applause when it was finished. Mayor Shuttlewood made a speech, then someone rang the clock tower bells. Ellen kept looking around for Carl but there was no sign of him, and she began to breathe easily again.

It was dark now, and snow was settling on the branches of the fir tree, coating the ornaments with a white powder that glowed in the gaslight from the street lamps. Ellen noticed the doves hovering around the nearby rooftops.

As people started to leave, Ellen realized her fingers and toes were numb with the cold. She and Mavis started up Newgate Street toward home, but then she saw a familiar-looking lorry parked opposite the Black Bull pub.

"Isn't that your dad's lorry?" Mavis asked.

"It looks like it." Ellen's mind was racing. What's Dad doing at the pub? He's supposed to be at home putting up the decorations. Has he forgotten it's Christmas Eve? Then she remembered his date with Len. Was there going to be trouble? She hoped he wasn't involved.

Just then a man came staggering out of the pub, obviously drunk.

"It's our Peter," Mavis gasped. She dashed across the road and grabbed her brother's arm. He tried to push her away, but she managed to get him back across the street with her. "Dad'll kill you," she said to Peter.

"Well th-that'll save me the b-b-bother," Peter stammered.

"Don't be daft — what are you saying?" Mavis said, looking embarrassed. She dragged Peter off in the direction of their home. "See you tomorrow, Ellen," she called back.

Ellen didn't know what to do. She had to talk to her dad and warn him that her mam was working for Geordie — especially if there was trouble brewing.

There were two or three men hanging around outside the pub, but no one she knew. Just then she saw Bobby walking down the street with a package under his arm. She ran up to him.

"Bobby, could you do me a favour?"

"Sure, what do you need?"

"It's my dad. I think he's in the pub, and I need to talk to him. I can't go in. Do you know any of those men outside? Could you ask them to nip in and ask him to come out?"

Bobby looked over at the men. "Yes — Andy Pickersgill's there. I'll ask him."

He went over and spoke to one of the men then came back to her. "Andy's gone to see if he's there. I have to be off. TTFN, Ellen. Have a good Christmas!"

Ellen stood stamping her feet to keep warm while she waited for her dad. Then the pub door swung open, and her dad came out carrying a large brown paper bag. Ellen ran up to him.

"I'm sorry, Dad. I —"

"What do you think you're doing? What do you mean by sending someone in to fetch me?" he demanded.

"It's Mam — she said you should know. She's working on the buses for Geordie Cruikshank. Mrs. Lumsden fell and broke her ribs, and me mam got her job and —"

"Your mam's what?"

"She's working as a conductress. It's only temporary."

"Well, that's a fine kettle of fish. I'll be back in a minute. You go climb into me lorry. Here, take the rabbit." He thrust the paper bag into her hands and went back into the pub.

Rabbit? Ellen peeked into the bag and felt sick as she saw the dead, furry rabbit. It must be for Christmas dinner. Her mam had been worried that they wouldn't have anything special. Ellen knew she wouldn't be able to eat any of it. Her mam hadn't cooked a rabbit since Squibs had died.

Poor Squibs. The pet rabbit had only lived a year after the Home Guard had found him safe and sound in the bottom of a dustbin after the bombing. Ellen had given him up for dead. Afterwards she realized that Carl must have put him in the dustbin to keep him safe from the falling debris. She'd never had the chance to thank Carl for that. She felt guilty now, thinking about how nasty she'd been to him back there at the clock tower.

What's me dad doing? Ellen wondered as she sat in the lorry waiting for him. Has he gone to stop Len from going after Geordie Cruikshank now that me mam's working for him? He won't let them hurt me mam, will he? Then she saw him coming back.

"Okay, that's settled. Now let's go home and get the decorations up. What time did you say your mam will be home?" he asked as he started up the lorry.

"Around eleven-thirty, but Dad — about Len —"

"Not a word to your mother. I don't know where Len got the rabbit, and I'm not asking any questions. I wasn't anywhere near the pub, all right?"

"Yes, Dad, all right," Ellen said. But she had a funny feeling it wasn't all right. If her dad had been in the pub to have a pint her mam might put up with that. But if it was anything to do with Geordie then there could be big trouble, and it wouldn't be all right at all.

10

Ellen was changing into her pyjamas when she heard her mam coming up the stairs to the flat. She glanced at the clock by the bed and saw it was almost midnight. Mam's late, Ellen thought, but she'll be pleased we got all the paper chains up and the presents put into the pillowcases.

The pillowcases, one for each of them, were always left on the hearth on Christmas Eve and were opened the next morning after breakfast. Ellen smiled to herself, imagining the look on Mavis's face when she saw what she had for her. She wondered what Mavis had got her. It was much more fun than buying something from the shops.

Her thoughts were suddenly interrupted by the sound of her dad shouting and she heard him run to the top of the stairs. She ran to see what was happening. Her dad had his arm around her mam's waist and was helping her up the stairs.

"What's happened, what've they done to you? Just wait till I get a hold of those louts," her dad shouted angrily.

"Mam, what's the matter? What —" Ellen stared at her mam. There was a nasty cut on her cheek, blood caked around her nose and one pocket of Sally's conductress uniform was ripped and hanging off.

"It's all right, pet; it looks worse than it is. I'm not hurt," Ellen's mam said.

"But what happened?" Ellen asked as she followed her mam and dad into the front room.

"Put the kettle on and make a cup of tea," Ellen's dad said as he helped her mam off with her coat. He sat her down in the leather chair near the fire and knelt beside her, rubbing her hands between his.

"Now, lass — tell us — who did this to you?" He reached out and touched her cheek, and as Ellen spooned the tea leaves into the teapot she heard her mam cry out in pain.

"Mam!" Ellen ran over to her.

"It's all right, love," her mam said. "It's nowt that a bit of iodine won't clear up. It was the crowd on the last bus. Noisy lot they were, joking and wise-cracking. It was all in good fun at first — you know how some of the men are when they've had a drop too much to drink. But then Geordie Cruikshank got on and they turned on him. Said he had no right to have POWs working for him."

"Who was on the bus?" Ellen's dad asked.

"Mostly men from the pubs. The rowdiest bunch got on at the Black Bull. The bus was full. Mavis's dad was there with some other men on the council, and it was pretty packed once that lot pushed their way on."

"Was Len with them?" Ellen's dad asked.

"Len? No, but that mate of his, Tommy whatshisname, was. What's Len got to with it? Is there something you're not telling me?"

"No, lass, of course not. Go on, what happened next?"

"A couple of people got mad and started yelling; then there was a lot of pushing and shoving. Next thing I knew, I was in the thick of it. By the time we got to the bus depot everyone was having a go."

Ellen stared at her mam in dismay. "You got into a fight? In front of everybody? And Mavis's dad was on the bus. Oh, Mam, you didn't!"

"Yes, I did, Ellen. And Mavis's dad's an old fart. He thinks there's still a war on."

"But, Mam, Mavis is my best friend."

"The kettle's boiling, our Ellen," her dad interrupted.

Ellen went to make the tea. She shuddered, thinking of Mavis's dad and the way he felt about the POWs. And what was the matter with her mam these days? First she was shouting and carrying on in the newsagent's last week, and now she was in a fight on the bus. It would be all over Morpeth tomorrow. And what would Mavis think? Ellen poured out three cups of tea, put them onto the wooden tray and carried it over to the fire.

"Well, that settles it. No more working on the buses for you," Ellen's dad said as Ellen handed her mam the tea.

"What! Don't be daft. You know we need the money. Besides, I'm not giving in to that lot. Why shouldn't Geordie employ who he wants? There's a chance he might take me on permanently, and if he does, I'm the one who'll decide if I'm to stay or not, thank you very much."

"We'll see about that."

Oh, please, don't start a row now, Ellen thought, not on Christmas Eve.

"Mam," she said. "Look, Dad and I got all the paper chains

up, and the pillowcases are ready, except for what you have to put in for us."

"Eeh, pet, so you have, and the place does look nice. I'll just put my presents in and we'll get off to bed. Now where did I put those socks I made for you?"

"Socks! Well, I hope you like the dishcloths I got for you," Ellen said sarcastically. She wondered what her mam *had* got for her. She knew she hadn't had time to knit a jumper.

"Dishcloths! How did you know what I wanted?"

"Oh, Mam, be serious."

"I am serious. Now be off with you. I have to nip down to Sally's first thing in the morning to tell her what happened and to see how she is. She seems a lot better now that she's seen the doctor, but she still needs some help with meals and dressing. If I'm not here when you get up you can start breakfast."

Ellen went back into her bedroom and snuggled under her covers, trying to keep warm. Why did her mam have to go running off to Sally's on Christmas morning? And why was she doing all these stupid things? Why couldn't she stay out of trouble and be an ordinary mother like Mavis's or Brenda's?

11

It took Ellen forever to fall asleep that night. When at last she did, she dreamt that Mavis's dad was chasing Carl around the clock tower with a giant Christmas tree in his hand. Nearby, her mam and dad were throwing snowballs at each other on top of a double-decker bus. Then the snowballs turned into doves, circling round and round her head, and suddenly she woke up. She was shivering. The eiderdown had slipped to the floor. Daylight was creeping in the window, and Ellen saw snowflakes swirling past the cracked window pane. She looked at the time: eight o'clock. It was Christmas morning!

She ate breakfast with her mam and dad after her mam got

back from Sally's, and then they opened their presents.

Ellen was still worried sick about what had happened on the bus the night before. Had Mavis's dad told her about the fight? If he had, then Ellen was sure Mavis wouldn't show up on Christmas Day as they had planned.

She was very relieved when Mavis arrived at one-thirty, just as they were finishing their Christmas dinner.

"Take your coat off, hinny, and come and sit by the fire," Ellen's mam said. "I'll make a nice cup of Ovaltine to warm you up."

The snow had stopped around noon, but heavy, dark clouds hung low in the sky, and a raw wind whistled in around the windows. Even the heat from the gas cooker, which Ellen's mam had used to roast the rabbit, hadn't warmed the flat much.

"That'd be nice," Mavis said. "I nearly froze to death getting here." When she took off her coat and head scarf Ellen noticed a large black beauty spot stuck on her cheek. Mavis saw her looking at it and grinned. "Do you like it?" she asked. "I've got two more and some super ones shaped like moons and stars. Brenda has some, too. You can have one if you want."

"Thanks." Brenda? Was Ellen losing her best friend?

"Daft idea if you ask me," Ellen's mam said as she handed Mavis her cup of Ovaltine.

"Oh, Mam, they're all the rage. Margaret Lockwood has them on in all her pictures."

"It's different for film stars. They can get away with wearing false teeth and eyelashes and dear knows what else." Ellen noticed her mam looking speculatively at Mavis's chest and realized Mavis's familiar yellow jumper seemed suddenly to have shrunk a size. She's gone and got one of those bullet brassieres, she thought. I'd better get her out of here before me mam comes out with any smart remarks.

"Come and see what Mam and Dad got me," she said, taking Mavis's arm and steering her toward her bedroom. Inside the tiny room Mavis sat on Ellen's bed, knees bent, arms hugged tightly around them.

"Brrr — it's cold in here," she said and pulled the eiderdown around her shoulders. Ellen reached under the mattress, opened the diary she kept there and took out the shiny silver pen from its spine.

"It's a Biro," she said proudly. Biros were the new pens that had just come on the market. Instead of a nib, they had a ball point to write with. As far as Ellen knew, no one else at school had one. They cost at least fifty shillings. She didn't know how her parents had managed to afford one when they said they didn't have enough money for a jumper, but she was thrilled to bits with it. She'd used it right away to write the latest entry in her diary this morning.

"A Biro!" Mavis looked impressed.

"Isn't it smashing?" Ellen asked.

"Yes, it's super, but I thought you were only exchanging homemade gifts or something that didn't cost much."

"We were, but me mam said she'd come into a bit of money. I think Geordie gave the conductresses an extra couple of quid for Christmas." She didn't add that her mam had also said she felt guilty that she hadn't had time to knit a jumper.

"Is it new?" Mavis asked.

"Of course. Why wouldn't it be?" Ellen was puzzled.

"No reason. Just there was one like it in the pawn shop window last week, and I thought I saw your mam going in there the other day. Not that it matters if she did get it there."

Ellen felt her face go red. Surely her mam and dad wouldn't give her a used pen! And certainly not one from the pawn shop. But her mam *had* said something about going to the pawn shop with that old silver tea set or her grandad's watch — or his medal. But her dad had mislaid the medal, hadn't he? Come to think about it, though, she hadn't seen the silver tea set on the sideboard for the last couple of days. No, her mam must have got the Biro somewhere else.

"My mam bought it at Appleby's — she told me," she lied.

"Well, it's great you've got it because you can use it on my gift right away — at least on January first." Mavis said as she handed Ellen the wrapped gift she'd brought into the bedroom.

"Wait, let me go first," Ellen said.

"No, let's toss for it. Here, I've got a penny. Heads or tails?" Mavis said throwing the coin into the air.

"Heads," Ellen said.

"Heads it is — you first."

"You'll never guess in a million years. I —"

"I know: it's a date with Bobby Forman!" Mavis interrupted.

"Don't be daft. It's something much better than that." Ellen took an envelope out of her dressing table drawer and handed it to Mavis.

"What is it?" Mavis asked as she opened it and took out the folded piece of paper.

"It's a pen friend — in Canada. Her name's Chris and she likes games and music. I got her name and address from *The People's Friend*. They have this section in the back of the magazine with names of people looking for pen friends. I've already written and asked her to write to you. You know I write to Shirley in Canada, and it's spiffing having a pen friend."

"I've never had a pen friend," Mavis said. "What's Shirley like?"

"She's really nice. We write to each other almost every week, and she's sending me some nylons. Her older sister, Joan, was over here during the war with the Canadian Forces, and she bumped into me dad one day in London. That's how we started writing."

"I wonder if Chris has an older brother." Mavis said.

"Well, you'll have to write and ask her, won't you? Now, what did you get for me?" Ellen asked as she carefully removed the brown wrapping paper from the package Mavis had given her. She gazed in surprise at the leather bound diary.

"It's lovely — but I thought we weren't going to spend money for gifts —"

"I didn't. Peter gave me one and then Brenda gave me another one, so as I don't need two, I thought . . ."

Brenda. Since when had Mavis and Brenda exchanged Christmas gifts? And which one had Mavis kept — the one from her brother or the one from Brenda?

"Now you can write about that boy you were dreaming about the other night — what was his name? Carl?"

"I told you, I don't know anybody called Carl." Ellen felt her heart pounding.

"No? What about Freda then; who's Freda?"

"Freda? What are you talking about?"

"I remembered afterwards — that was another name you said in your sleep. I think you're mean not telling me. Best friends don't keep secrets from each other."

"I'm not keeping any secrets from you. I don't know anybody called Carl or anybody called Freda, and I don't want to talk about this anymore." Before Mavis could say another word, Ellen said, "Thank you for the diary. I'll be back in a minute. I have to go to the lav."

She hurried from the bedroom, grabbed her coat from the top of the stairs and ran down and out across the yard to the lavs. She needed a moment to think. I bet she told Brenda I didn't have any money for presents, Ellen thought. I hope she didn't tell Brenda that Sally Lumsden gave me that bottle of Evening in Paris. If she did, I'd just die.

If only Mavis would stop keeping on at her about Carl. And who was Freda? Then she realized it wasn't Freda. It was Elfreida, Carl's little sister — the one he'd said Ellen reminded him of. I've got to get Mavis thinking about something else, Ellen thought. Then she realized she knew just what to say to distract her friend. She pulled the lavatory chain then ran back across the yard and upstairs to her bedroom.

"Mavis, did Bobby . . ." Horrified, Ellen stopped in the bedroom doorway. Mavis was sitting on the bed, Ellen's old diary open on her lap.

"Give me that!" Ellen lunged at her, grabbing the journal. "How dare you read my diary! How dare you!"

"I wasn't reading it. I moved the pillow and it fell on the floor."

"Don't lie to me! You were reading it. I saw you."

"I'm not lying. I just wondered if it was full and if you really needed the new one I gave you. That's all."

"You had no right. It's private."

"Well, pardon me. If that's the way you feel you can keep your silly old pen friend! Who wants to waste time writing letters to strangers anyway?" Mavis scrunched up the paper Ellen had given her and flung it onto the bed.

"It's better than wasting time chasing after Bobby Forman when he's not interested."

"You're just jealous. And you need talk — 'I don't know anyone called Carl,'" she mimicked.

What did that mean? Ellen felt the familiar panicky feeling in her chest. What had Mavis read in her diary? She knew she shouldn't have written *anything* about Carl, but it had been the only place she'd felt safe talking about him.

Just then Ellen's mam put her head around the door. "I hate to break things up, girls, but it's snowing again and looks as if it means business. Maybe you should be heading home, Mavis, before it gets too bad."

"Yes, I'd better get going," Mavis agreed.

She didn't say anything to Ellen as she put on her coat and head scarf and headed off down the stairs. Ellen ran to the front room window and bit on her lip to stop herself from crying as she watched her friend stomp off along the snowy street below.

"What's the matter with Mavis?" her mam asked. "She seemed upset."

"Nothing. We had a bit of an argument. She'll be all right the next time I see her." But Ellen wondered if that was true. They'd been friends forever, and they'd never had a fight before.

12

As Ellen hung up her coat in the school cloakroom on the first day back from the Christmas holidays, she looked around for Mavis — half hoping she'd be home sick.

For the first few days after their fight, Ellen had thought Mavis would come around to the flat like she always had over the holidays. When she didn't, Ellen had set off one day for her house. She'd turned back when she'd seen Mavis going into Woolworths with Brenda.

Then she'd hoped they might bump into each other at the New Year's Eve celebrations. Everybody always gathered at the clock tower at midnight to sing "Auld Lang Syne" and hear the tower bells ring in the New Year. But it had been bitterly cold and windy that night and not many people turned up. Ellen had gone with her mam and dad, but there'd been no sign of Mavis.

Now, as Ellen shook the snow from her wellies and changed into her shoes, she heard laughter. Her heart missed a beat as she saw Mavis, along with Brenda and two other girls, over by the door to the gym. They were looking at a newspaper and hadn't seen her. Should she go over to them? In her mind she'd practised a hundred times what she was going to say to Mavis: that she was sorry, that she hadn't meant what she'd said. Fiddling with her schoolbag, she edged closer, staying out of sight behind the coats, trying to hear what the girls were saying.

"I didn't believe it when me dad showed me the paper this morning," Brenda giggled. "I'd just die if my mother did a thing like that."

"Me, too," one of the other girls said. "And why would anyone stand up for those awful POWs?"

Just then the bell rang, and they all hurried off to the gym for morning assembly. What was that about? Ellen wondered. As she crossed to follow them, she caught sight of the newspaper lying on the bench.

She hung back till all the other girls had gone; then she picked up the paper. It was the *Morpeth Weekly,* and on the front page, in large black type, was the headline, *HOLIDAY FRACAS ON LOCAL BUS — COUNCILLOR GETS BLACK EYE.* Underneath was a picture of a woman hitting a man over the head with what looked like a bag. Ellen gasped as she realized the woman was her mother and the man was Mavis's father! Me mam hit Mavis's dad! she thought, horrified.

Quickly, she glanced through the accompanying article: "Fight Over Prisoners of War." There was a quote from Mavis's dad: "The attack was completely unwarranted. I stand by my position on the prisoners of war. They are not welcome here — they should be sent back to Germany where they belong and not be employed by local farmers and businessmen. Those Nazis killed and maimed our brave soldiers. People should not have anything to do with them, and any Nazi sympathizer should be firmly dealt with." Nazi sympathizer? Is that what people thought about her mam? Is that what they would think of her if the truth came out about Carl?

Ellen could hear the opening hymn coming from the gym. What'll I do? she thought. I can't go in there, I just can't.

She flung the paper down and grabbed her coat, pushing her arms into the sleeves as she ran out the door and across the courtyard to the street. She was halfway home when she realized her feet were soaking, that she hadn't changed back into her wellies. As she ran down Beeswing Yard and up the stairs to the flat, her mind was racing. How could me mam do this to me? Mavis was laughing! They were all laughing! And what had Mavis's dad said about it? That whoever sympathized with the POWs should be firmly dealt with! Had Mavis read about Carl in her diary? Had she told her dad about it?

"What are you doing home? Why aren't you at school?" Ellen's mam stood at the top of the stairs, holding her coat.

"Why didn't you tell me you hit Mavis's dad and that your picture was all over the front page of the paper? I'll never be able to face any of my friends again!" Ellen shouted at her.

"What? What are you talking about?"

"You and that fight you had on the bus. There's a picture in the paper of you hitting Mavis's dad. And everyone's calling you a Nazi sympathizer."

"Calm down. The war's over and there's two sides to every story. Somebody has to stick up for the underdog."

"Well, why does it have to be you? Why can't you be normal like everyone else's mother?"

"That's enough. I did what I thought was right. We'll talk about this when you get home from school this afternoon.

Now you'd better get on back. You've already missed assembly."

"I'm not going back. I'm not ever going back, and you can't make me."

"Oh, yes, I can. There's many a one would give their right arm to be at that school. Now, we're almost out of coal, and I'm going out to see if I can find some. You'd best be gone by the time I get back." With that she put on her coat and head scarf and went out.

Ellen sat by the fire, huddled over the dying embers to keep warm. She hadn't really meant it when she'd said she was never going back to school. She knew she couldn't do that. Besides, she loved school — or at least she had up till now.

She heard the postman put the mail through the letter box and ran downstairs, scooped up the envelopes and rifled through them. Mostly bills. Oh good, there was another letter from Canada. She took it back to the armchair by the fire to read.

Dear Ellen,

Thank you for your letter. I was surprised to hear
that you are having lots of snow. Of course we
have mountains of it here every winter. My dad is
teaching me how to ski. My sister says your country

is very beautiful but everything is so small. My parents
are very happy about us writing to each other. They
want to know if there is anything else you would like us
to send you. Is there? I'm glad you liked the soap. Have
the nylons arrived yet? It's hard to imagine things being
rationed so long after the war. We have plenty of food
and all kinds of clothes here. I hope your father finds a
job soon. Your mother's job sounds nice — it must be
fun working on a bus and meeting all kinds of people.
Please write back soon.

Your friend,

Shirley

Oh, it's fun having your mother work on a bus all right. Especially if you want to lose all your friends, Ellen thought. But at least she still had Shirley.

Ellen got a blue airmail letter and her new Biro pen and sat down to write back. First she answered Shirley's questions; then she found herself telling her all about the fight with Mavis, but of course she didn't mention Carl. She told her about her dad still looking for work, and she even told her about the window being stuck open in the living room and the snow blowing in.

Shirley may never write to me again when she reads this

tale of woe, Ellen thought. Maybe I shouldn't send it. Before she could change her mind, she sealed the blue airmail letter and ran and posted it in the mailbox at the corner.

When she got back to the flat, her dad was sitting by the empty fireplace, his coat still on, and his head in his hands. The *Morpeth Weekly* lay at his feet.

"You've seen it, then," Ellen said as her dad looked up.

"Aye, I've seen it all right. What are you doing home at this time of day?"

"I couldn't stay at school. Everybody's laughing."

"It's no laughing matter. Somebody's out to make trouble, putting this in the paper. But that's no excuse for you staying home. Now get yourself back," Ellen's dad said.

"But, Dad, I can't —"

"Look, our Ellen, I've got enough to worry about right now. I said get back to school and I meant it. We'll talk about this tonight. Where's your mam?"

"She went out to find some coal."

"By herself?"

"Yes, I think so."

"Then I'd better go and look for her. The crowd in the unemployment office this morning was getting a bit ugly over the POWs doing work they could be doing. I wouldn't want her to run into any of that lot right now. You've missed your lunch at school. Better get something to eat before you go back."

Ellen couldn't stop from shivering from the cold as she made herself a Spam sandwich. She couldn't go back to school, she just couldn't. But if she stayed home her mam and dad would be mad. Slowly she put on her coat and head scarf and went outside. Wet sleet was falling, and the sky was dark and heavy. She crossed the road and walked toward the school, still not sure how she could bring herself go to inside. So instead of opening the gates, she just kept on going.

13

I'm not going back — not today anyhow, she decided. I'll say I was sick and maybe by tomorrow they'll have forgotten all about it. If I stay out till four o'clock, no one will know I haven't been to school, but I'll have to watch out for Mam. Though, if she's looking for coal, she shouldn't be in this part of town.

Ellen decided to go to the library at Boots. She'd joined it a year ago when it had first opened in the back room of the chemist's shop. It cost sixpence to join, but it had newer books than the public library. Today the small secluded room was deserted.

Ellen found a book in the Abbey School series, by Elsie J.

Oxenham, one she hadn't read, and sat down in one of the library armchairs. But she couldn't keep her mind on it. She kept thinking about her friends laughing at her mam.

She could also hear, but not see, customers coming and going at the dispensary counter that was just outside the library door. She was half-listening to people chatting about the weather, complaining about the snow and the cold, when a familiar voice caught her attention. It was Mavis's dad.

"I'll take some of that Sloane's liniment, too. My back's not been right since that to-do on the bus the other night."

"Yes, I read about it in the paper," the man behind the counter replied. "After all we've been through with the war, you'd think people could find better ways of solving things than by fighting with each other."

"Aye, well, if Geordie Cruikshank keeps on using those POWs, there'll be a lot more trouble, you mark my words."

Ellen heard the clink of the cash register being opened and closed; then the chemist said, "I feel sorry for Geordie — he's only trying to run a business."

"Hmph, I wouldn't waste my time feeling sorry for the likes of him, if I was you. He's asking for it," Mavis's dad said. "Hobnobbing with the enemy the way he is. I'll never forgive them for what they've done to our Peter."

"He's not any better then?"

"No, and he's not likely to be for a long time from the looks of things. He's a hero, you know — got a King's medal to prove it."

Ellen heard the tinkle of the shop doorbell as Mavis's dad left. Her hands were shaking as she put down the book she'd been trying to read and looked at the clock on the wall. Three thirty — half an hour to go before she could go home. She was tired of sitting still. She decided to have a look in the record shop.

She was within sight of the door to the shop when she saw her mother coming up Oldgate toward her, head lowered against the biting wind. Oh, no, I mustn't let her see me, Ellen thought, looking desperately for somewhere to hide. Then she noticed that the narrow wooden door at the bottom of the clock tower was slightly ajar. Quickly, she slipped inside and pulled the door closed behind her. She'd never been inside the tower before, and as her eyes adjusted to the dim light coming from slits high in the walls, she saw an iron spiral staircase leading upward to the clock and the belfry.

Shivering, she sat on the bottom step and looked around her. The thick walls of the tower blocked out all the outside noises, and the place smelled of damp. As her eyes became accustomed to the dark, she noticed a pile of straw in the far corner and a brown paper bag with some crusts of bread lying beside it. Was someone here? Fearfully, she looked around, but there was no sign of anybody.

She made herself count to sixty ten times. Me mam should be gone by now, she thought, as she went to the door to lift the latch. But the door wouldn't open. She pulled harder but still it wouldn't budge. Now what was she going to do?

She was shaking and it wasn't just with the cold. Memories of the bomb, screaming, walls closing in, flashed into her mind. A sharp jab of fear grabbed her stomach, and in spite of the cold she began to sweat. Don't be daft, she told herself. There's no bomb; the war's over, remember?

Ellen tried to think of what to do next. She *could* ring the bells, but that would bring the whole town running — the bells were only rung on Sundays or on special occasions — and she didn't want that. I'll wait a bit longer, maybe someone will show up, she thought. Or, perhaps if I go further up I could shout through one of the openings in the walls and get someone in the street to let me out.

She began climbing the stairs and was halfway up when there was a rustling noise from above. Heart racing, she paused, straining to hear. Was something, or someone, up there? But now she couldn't hear anything except the pounding of her heart.

She stood rigid for a minute, and then she started moving up again. As she climbed higher she could barely make out the platform around the clock, and when she reached it she saw the slits in the walls were very narrow. There was more light coming from above, so she decided to climb on up to the belfry. Long bell pulls hung like silent ghosts, and Ellen got a creepy feeling up the back of her neck. She'd almost reached the top when some of the light suddenly disappeared. Looking up she saw the silhouette of a figure looming above her, and she screamed. Then someone shouted, "Who's that? Ellen? Hey, it's only me . . ." and the light came back as the figure bent down toward her. Ellen gasped as she recognized Bobby Forman.

"You scared the living daylights out of me," she snapped. "What are you doing here?"

"Sorry," he said. "You startled me, too. Come on up, and I'll show you."

Curious, Ellen climbed the rest of the stairs and stood beside him on the platform. He gestured to one of the window-like openings in the wall, and Ellen peered out. On the windswept streets below, people were scurrying between the shops. One of Cruikshank's buses was pulling out of the marketplace onto Bridge Street.

"No — there — look," Bobby said pointing to the Christmas tree beside the tower.

"What?" Ellen asked.

"At the top of the tree. Over there, to the right." Ellen looked and saw a nest with a dove sitting on it.

"There's two eggs in it. I've been watching for a while. She'll lose them when they take the tree down."

"Me mam said doves wouldn't be daft enough to make a nest in the Christmas tree. It looks as if she was wrong."

"My science teacher let me out early to take pictures," Bobby said, pointing to the Brownie box camera slung around his neck. "I'm getting up a petition to stop them taking the tree down. Have to present it at the next Town Hall Meeting. I've got pigeons of my own, you know. But what are you doing here?"

"Nothing. I-I just popped in to get out of the wind for a bit. The door's stuck closed. I couldn't get back out."

"It does that all the time," Bobby said. "There's a knack to it. I'll show you."

Gingerly, Ellen climbed down the staircase after him, and when they got to the bottom he wiggled the latch, shoved the door with his shoulder and it popped open. As they stepped out into the biting wind, Ellen put her hand on his arm and said, "Thanks, Bobby."

"It was nowt. Maybe you could sign my petition?" he said, looking embarrassed. He pulled a piece of paper from his bag.

"Of course," Ellen said, signing her name.

"Thanks, Ellen. See you later," he said, smiling. Then he strode off along Oldgate toward home.

Fancy him being so interested in doves, Ellen thought as she pulled her coat collar up around her ears. Maybe he wasn't such a drip after all.

As she turned to face the driving wind, she glanced across the street and got a sinking feeling in her stomach. There was Mavis, glowering at her from the doorway of the music shop.

14

"Mavis! Wait!" Ellen shouted as she ran across the street, but Mavis had turned her back on her and was opening the music shop door.

Just as Ellen reached her, Mavis turned around and hissed, "Traitor." Then she was gone, into the shop, slamming the door behind her.

Stunned, Ellen stared after her. What did she mean, "traitor"? Was she talking about Carl, or was she mad because she thought Ellen had been out with Bobby? Ellen wondered if she should go after Mavis, but she didn't want to have another fight with her — not in the music shop, in front of everyone.

I know, she decided, I'll go to school early tomorrow and try and catch her before assembly.

Ellen couldn't get Mavis out of her mind as she ran toward Beeswing Yard. If she hadn't read my diary we wouldn't have had that stupid row, she thought. We'd still be best friends. And it wouldn't matter so much about everyone laughing at me mam if Mavis was still me best friend. I'd just die if she told anyone about Carl, though. She wouldn't, would she? But Mavis had looked so angry standing there in the music shop doorway.

Brushing the snow from her coat, Ellen pushed open the door to the flat. As she closed it, she heard angry voices, and all thoughts of Mavis flew from her head. Her mam and dad were having a row.

Hoping it wasn't about her skipping school, Ellen reluctantly climbed the stairs. But her parents were too busy yelling at each other to notice her as she hesitated in the doorway.

"I said you're to give up the job, and that's all there is to it." Ellen's dad was standing in front of the fireplace, legs apart, wagging a finger at her mam.

"Just try and make me. If Geordie gets his licence renewed he's going to take me on full-time. I'm not letting him down now." Ellen's mam slammed the cups and saucers on the table.

"I told you — there's going to be trouble; he shouldn't have given you the job. You'll only be able to work for a few more months anyhow, and if there's trouble, it's not safe for you in your condition."

"Geordie doesn't know about my 'condition.' Besides, I can take care of myself."

Condition? What were they talking about? Why could her mam only work for a few more months? A picture of her retching into the chamber pot flashed into Ellen's head. Was there something wrong with her mam? Was she? No, she couldn't be. She was too old to be expecting. Her mam was almost forty. Women that old didn't have babies, did they?

"Mam —" She struggled out of her wet coat as she stepped into the room. "What's the matter?"

"Oh, you gave me a fright, our Ellen. I didn't hear you come in." Her mam went over to the sideboard to get some plates. "Come and sit down. I want to talk to you, young lady. Where have you been?"

"Wh-what do you mean?" Ellen stammered. Her knees felt wobbly as she sat down at the table.

"You know what I mean. I met the school secretary on the street. You weren't at school today. Where were you?"

"I-I-I didn't feel well. I went to Boots — to the library."

"So, you were well enough to read but not to do arithmetic and Latin? You don't realize, my girl, how lucky you are to be at that school. Don't you ever do that again, do you hear? Now, what are you going to do about it?"

"Do?"

"Yes, do," Ellen's mam snapped.

"I-I — would you give me a note?"

"No, I will not give you a note. You'll go to Miss Blackthorn first thing tomorrow morning and apologize."

"What! Why won't you give me a note? Mavis's mam said *she* was sick when they went shopping in Newcastle. Why won't you?"

"I'm not Mavis's mam, and —"

"Eeh, hinny, don't be so hard on the bairn," Ellen's dad interrupted.

"I'm not being hard. She's not a bairn, and she has to learn to be responsible for her actions."

"It was all because of you and your stupid actions that I did it!" Ellen shouted. "Everyone was laughing at me because you were in the paper hitting Mavis's dad."

"Were they now?" Ellen's mam said. "Well I was only standing up for what I thought was right, and I'll not have you using me as an excuse. Now have your tea; I've got to get to work."

She yanked her coat from the peg and rammed the conductress cap on her head.

"You're going then?" Ellen's dad asked. "You're not taking any notice of what I said?"

"No, I'm not," Ellen's mam snapped. "I'm not going to let a bunch of stupid drunks scare me out of a perfectly good job. There's shepherd's pie in the oven. I'll be back around eleven-thirty." She ran off down the stairs, and Ellen's dad went over to the window and stood looking down into the street, shaking his head.

"She's a stubborn woman, your mother," he said. "I'd better go and keep an eye on Len and his mates."

"Why doesn't Len like Mr. Cruikshank?" Ellen asked.

"Well, pet, that's a complicated story. Len says it's because Geordie doesn't have to pay the POWs much money, so he doesn't hire anybody who really needs a job — like Len and myself — because we'd cost more."

"But he took Alfie Jones on — and me mam."

"Yes, but the prisoners can't drive the buses, and he was stuck for a driver. As for your mam, Len says Geordie keeps the women on because he can get away with paying them less than he'd have to pay a man."

As he put on his coat, Ellen said, "Dad — is there something the matter with me mam? She's not sick, is she?"

"Sick? She's stubborn and headstrong, but I wouldn't go so far as to say she was sick. Not your mam."

"I didn't mean that. You said something about her 'condition?'"

He looked embarrassed, and Ellen was surprised when he turned away and walked to the top of the stairs without answering.

"Dad?"

He hesitated, then turned to look at her. "I suppose I might as well tell you — you'll know soon enough, anyhow. She's in the family way."

"She's what?" Ellen still couldn't believe it.

"She's in the family way. She's having a bairn. That's why she's been a bit out of sorts lately. So no more playing hooky, pet. She's got more than enough on her mind right now."

Ellen stood gaping after him as he dashed down the stairs and out the door. So it *was* true. She should have known. She remembered the way her mam had snapped at her when she'd said that Sally's uniform was too tight. And the white knitting wool — her mam had tried to hide it from her, hadn't she?

She went to the sideboard and flung open the bottom drawer, tossing things aside, looking for her mam's knitting bag. She found it in the corner and yanked it out, fumbling with the drawstring. There, staring up at her, were two balls of soft white wool and a tiny, half-knitted jacket. She carried it over to the leather armchair by the fire and sat gazing into the flames. It was true then. But they didn't have room for a baby! Where would it sleep? And what would her friends say? A few of the girls in her class had younger brothers or sisters, but they were only a couple of years younger. No one had a *baby* brother or sister.

Suddenly she felt angry. Why did her mam have to have a baby? Why couldn't she be like everyone else's mother? "I don't want a stupid baby brother or sister!" she yelled, ripping the wool from the needles. "I want me dad to have a steady job, me mam to stay home and Carl to go back to Germany. And I want to still be friends with Mavis and . . . and . . ." She tugged angrily at the tiny jacket, pulling out the neatly worked stitches row by row, until all that was left was a heap of tangled crinkly yarn.

15

As the dying embers shifted, Ellen shivered and leaned closer to the fire trying to catch the last of their glowing warmth. The room had grown dark, and as the clock chimed six, she realized she'd been sitting there, staring into the fire, for almost an hour. The words "she's having a bairn" kept going round and round in her head. She was suddenly aware of a knocking sound and realized someone was at the door.

Wondering who it could be, she switched on the hall light and slowly made her way down the stairs. She pulled the door open and gasped in surprise — there was Mavis, standing on the step.

"Mavis, come in! I-I — "

"I can't stay," Mavis interrupted as she stepped into the hallway. She seemed agitated. "I just wanted to know — are we still friends?"

"Friends? Of course we are. Listen, about me mam hitting your dad —"

To Ellen's surprise, Mavis started to laugh. "I thought it was funny. So did me mam. Said me dad should have more sense than to get into a drunken fight over something he can't do anything about."

The awful feeling of despondency that had gripped Ellen since that morning eased off a bit. "And about Bobby —"

"I was mad at first, but honestly . . . there was this smashing new bloke at the youth club the other night. I'd almost forgotten about Bobby until I saw him with you."

Well, fancy that, Ellen thought. And here I've been worrying meself sick over it.

"Are you coming in?" she asked Mavis.

"No. I can't. I'm on my way to my piano lesson. I can't skip it — my dad's in enough of a flap. Someone stole our Peter's medal. Dad's sure it was one of the POWs, but there wasn't any sign of a break-in and nothing else was taken. Just the smashed frame and broken glass were left behind."

Ellen felt her heartbeat quicken at the mention of the POWs. *Had* Mavis read about Carl in her diary?

"Anyway," Mavis said. "I just wanted to see you and make sure we were still friends. I've felt just awful since our fight. I swear I didn't look at your diary that day. Cross my heart and hope to die."

"Thanks, Mavis. I'm glad we're still friends."

"I've got to run now. But I'll see you tomorrow?" Mavis said, giving Ellen a quick hug.

Ellen watched her go up the yard to the street, and then she closed the door and climbed back up the stairs to the flat. She thought about what had just happened. It felt so good to be friends with Mavis again, but was she telling the truth about not reading the diary? She seemed so sincere. And if she had read it, she would have told someone by now, wouldn't she?

There were footsteps on the stairs, and Ellen realized her dad was back. Quickly, she shoved the pile of unravelled wool under the chair, grabbed a book from the nearby table and pretended to be reading.

"Eeh, lass, you'll catch your death sitting here in the cold. Put a cardigan or something on, and I'll make us a warm cup of cocoa."

Ellen went to her room, got her dressing gown and put it on

over her blouse and skirt. When she went back to the living room her dad was pouring scalded milk into mugs.

"There we are. What a day. I think everybody's gone daft," he said, stirring the hot liquid.

"What do you mean?"

"Oh, it's nowt for you to worry about, but I wouldn't want to be in Geordie Cruikshank's shoes. Somebody threw a brick through his garage window, and Len and a few of the men were all set to pelt the buses with stones till I managed to talk some sense into them. And they're determined to go to the meeting tomorrow night — the one about the bus licence renewal — and cause trouble."

"Oh, no, how awful. What do you think about all this, Dad?"

"Eeh, hinny, I don't know. I'm stuck right in the middle, not having a job and your mam working for Geordie. Len's got a point, but violence is no way to solve things. There's two sides to every story, and it's not easy to get everybody to see them. Sometimes if you stand up for what you believe in you get hurt, and I don't want to see that happen to your mam, especially not right now."

There was an awkward silence. Ellen knew he meant because of the baby. She wanted to ask him when it was due and if he wanted a boy or a girl, but he turned on the wireless and started fidgeting with the newspaper, as if he didn't want to talk any more.

"I'm going to write to Shirley," she said and escaped to her room. She wanted to tell her about being friends with Mavis again. Then she told her about the baby. It seemed easier somehow to tell someone she'd never met, rather than Mavis and her friends at school. As she slipped out to post the letter, she noticed her dad was sitting staring into the fire, the paper still on his lap.

When she got back she went straight to bed, but she couldn't fall asleep. She was afraid that if she did, she'd have another of those dreadful nightmares. Who had stolen Peter's medal? she wondered. And why just the medal? There were lots of other valuable things in Mavis's house.

Maybe it *was* one of the POWs — taking the one thing that had been given for killing a German — one of their own. They'd probably heard Mr. Ramsbottom boasting about it all over town.

We're supposed to be at peace, so why can't everyone get along? Ellen wondered. Why can't people forgive and forget?

16

Ellen woke up the next morning with a feeling of dread. Instead of huddling under the covers for a few extra minutes, as she usually did, she ran to the window, scraped a hole in the frost on the inside of the glass, and peered anxiously out.

Please God, she prayed, let it have snowed all night so that I won't have to go to school. She felt sick at the thought of having to tell Miss Blackthorn she'd played hooky.

But although the sky was heavy and dark, there wasn't much more snow on the ground than there had been yesterday.

Oh well, at least Mavis was speaking to her again.

"Ellen, breakfast's ready. Are you up?" Ellen heard her mam shout from the kitchen.

"Yes — coming." Thoughts tumbled through her head as she struggled into her blouse, fumbling with the buttons: I don't want to talk to Miss Blackthorn — I can't. What am I going to do? She yanked her gym tunic over her head, quickly ran a comb through her hair, grabbed her coat and schoolbag and dashed from the room.

"I've got to go, Mam. There's a choir practice — I forgot I have to be there early."

"Oh, why didn't you tell me? Here, take an egg sandwich with you. And don't forget now, you're to tell Miss Blackthorn why you weren't at school yesterday."

"Oh, Mam, do I have to? Couldn't you —"

"No, I couldn't, and yes, you do. Telling the truth's important. I'm not saying it's easy, but it's always best in the long run. Now off you go."

No, it's not always best, Ellen thought as she trudged through the snow up the yard. When she got to school a few moments later, she had to force herself to go through the gates.

"Oh, there you are." Ellen turned from hanging her coat up in the cloakroom to find herself facing Miss Blackthorn. "I was just checking the attendance sheets and saw you were away yesterday, Ellen. Were you ill? You don't look too well. Come on into my study and we'll have a little chat."

Oh, no, she thinks I was sick. How am I going to tell her? Ellen wondered as she followed the headmistress into her study.

"I've been a little concerned about you the last few days, Ellen," Miss Blackthorn motioned her into a chintz-covered chair. "I know there's been some talk about your mother."

Ellen cringed. So even Miss Blackthorn knew about the fight on the bus and the picture in the paper.

"Classmates can sometimes be cruel," the headmistress continued, "and I want you to know that I, personally, admire your mother for standing up for what she believes in. Not that I approve of her hitting Mr. Ramsbottom, mind you."

Ellen stared at Miss Blackthorn in surprise. Was she trying not to smile?

"Now, about yesterday?"

Ellen took a deep breath. "I-I went to Boots. To the library, instead of coming to school. I'm sorry. I couldn't face everybody. I won't do it again." There, it was out. She bit her lip and looked down at her feet.

"I'm sorry, too, but I'm glad you told me. You realize, of course, there will have to be some kind of punishment." Miss

Blackthorn stood up and took a book from one of the many shelves lining the study walls. "Yes, this will do nicely. I want you to read this and any others you can find on the subject, and write me a ten page composition about it. I'd like to have it by the week after next. Now — I believe you have choir practice." She handed Ellen the book and nodded her dismissal.

"Th-thank you," Ellen stammered as she hurried from the room. Was that all? A ten page composition? That wasn't so bad. And fancy her saying that about me mam, Ellen thought as she went back to the cloakroom to collect her schoolbag. As she thrust the book inside her bag, she glanced at the title: *Emmeline Pankhurst and the Suffragette Movement.* Suffragette movement? Wasn't that something about women getting the vote? She was about to take a closer look at the book when Mavis came running into the cloakroom.

"Ellen — you'll never guess what's happened."

Oh, no, what now? Ellen wondered.

"I got a letter from that pen friend you got me in Canada. Chris is a boy, not a girl! He said you'd written asking him to be sure and write to me and he did. He sent a photo and he's smashing — here, look."

She thrust a snapshot in front of Ellen. Chris was indeed

smashing — tall and slim with blond hair and a lopsided grin. The awful tension that had gripped Ellen these last few weeks eased off a bit. Maybe things were going to be all right after all. Miss Blackthorn hadn't expelled her, and Mavis was still her best friend. Now if she could just get Carl out of her life everything would be okay again.

17

But when Ellen got home from school that afternoon, her mam and dad were shouting at each other again. She realized her problems were far from over. She stood, listening, halfway up the stairs.

"You're out of your mind swapping shifts to go to that meeting! It's going to be a free-for-all. And how do you think it's going to look to Len and the lads if you show up? It's bad enough that me wife's working for Geordie Cruikshank, without you saying he should be allowed to hire the POWs if he wants," Ellen's dad yelled.

"Somebody has to support Geordie. It's not just Len

— there's that bus man from Newcastle. I heard he's even bribed some of the councillors to vote for him. Ramsbottom will vote against Geordie for sure — he hates his guts."

"And what do you think *you* can do about that?"

"I don't know. I only know I've got to be there. Please try to understand. Look, I promise I'll keep out of trouble."

"I don't have much say in the matter, do I? You'll do what you want anyhow. But just remember that if you make a fuss, neither of us will work again in this town for a very long time."

"I'm not daft. I'm not going to do anything stupid."

Oh, no, Ellen thought as she climbed on up the rest of the stairs and stood at the doorway to the living room. If me mam goes to that meeting, I know she won't be able to keep her mouth shut. Why can't she just let them fight it out amongst themselves?

"Oh, there you are, Ellen," her mam said. "There's some broth on the cooker. The tap's frozen again, so go easy on the water, will you?"

Ellen watched in a daze as her mam hurried off down the stairs. She went to the cooker and warmed up the broth, then filled two soup bowls. Her dad was just standing at the window, staring out again.

"Do you want a cup of tea, Dad?" she asked.

"What?"

"Tea — do you want some?"

"No, hinny, and I'm not hungry. I'd better go and see if I can talk some sense into Len and the others before the meeting. Don't wait up. It could be a long night."

After he'd gone, Ellen tried to eat but found she wasn't hungry either. How badly did Geordie Cruikshank want to keep the bus route? Enough to get rid of the POWs? Would any of them be at the meeting? What would happen if her mam caused a fuss? She pushed the thoughts from her mind and started to write in her diary, but her heart wasn't in it. After a while she put it aside.

Then she got the book on suffragettes from her schoolbag and began reading it. At first she couldn't concentrate. Her eyes were reading the words but her mind was thinking of different ones — Carl, Mavis's dad, Geordie Cruikshank, the meeting, her mother, the baby. She'd almost forgotten about the baby. She wondered who it would look like and what they'd call it. She kept looking at the clock and wondering if she dared go to the meeting.

But after a while she got caught up in the story of Emmeline Pankhurst. To get the vote for women, she'd gone on hunger strikes and had even gone to prison. She's a bit like me mam,

Ellen thought. Funny, I always thought me mam was different from everybody else. I never knew there were others who could feel the way she does about things. Mrs. Pankhurst's daughters weren't the least bit ashamed of her, either, not like Ellen was sometimes of her mam. They'd even been sent to prison themselves for helping her.

There was another famous suffragette, Emily Wilding Davison, and Ellen was surprised to read that she came from Morpeth and was buried right here in the churchyard. She'd thrown herself in front of a horse on Derby Day to try to get people to listen. I must go and look for her grave sometime, Ellen thought.

She looked at the clock again and saw it was a quarter to seven. The meeting would be starting soon, but the council would probably have other things to talk about before getting to the bus licence. Her mam and dad would be mad if she went to the meeting, but anything was better than sitting here in this cold empty room, waiting and wondering what might happen. I'm going, she decided.

Outside, snow was falling so heavily she could hardly see in front of her. She pulled her head scarf tightly around her ears and bent her head into the storm. There was sheer ice underneath the snow, and she stumbled and almost fell several times as she headed down Newgate Street toward the town hall.

The streets were deserted, but as she passed the clock tower she felt someone grab her arm. As she was pulled toward the small wooden door at the base of the tower, she started to scream. But a rough hand suddenly covered her mouth, and she was dragged into the tower.

"Don't be 'fraid *Fräulein* Ellen — it is me, Carl," the voice said. He let go of her, closed the door behind them and switched on the dim light.

Ellen angrily spun around to face him. "What do you think you're doing? I told you — leave me alone!"

"Here —" he held something out toward her. "It was in the pocket of the coat you gave to me. I thought you should want it back."

Dumbfounded, Ellen stared at what he was holding out to her. It looked like a medal. Was it? Could it be her grandfather's medal? The one her dad had lost? Carl had said it was in the pocket of her dad's coat — the coat she'd given to him to help him escape from the Home Guard. No wonder her dad couldn't find it.

"Oh, thank you, thank you! You've saved my dad's bacon."

"Bacon? What is dad's bacon?"

She burst out laughing. "It's —"

Suddenly the door burst open and in came Mavis's dad. Ellen jumped and quickly stepped back from Carl.

"What's going on here? What are you doing? I saw you force Ellen in here — are you hurt, girl? And what have you got there?" Mavis's dad demanded. The medal was still in Carl's hand. Carl cringed and took a step backwards, losing his balance and dropping the medal. Mr. Ramsbottom bent to pick it up, and Ellen watched in fear as his expression changed from curiosity to anger. Red-faced, he yelled, "It's Peter's medal! You stole my son's medal. I knew it was one of you beggars. You Nazi — you! We'll see what the police have to say about this." He grabbed Carl's arm and twisted it behind his back.

"You're coming with me to the police station. But first we're going to that meeting at the town hall. This'll settle Geordie Cruikshank and his POWs once and for all. I told him they were a thieving lot of bastards. Now I've got proof."

"No — wait!" Ellen tried to get his attention.

"Quiet, girl. You're just lucky I spotted him dragging you in here — dear knows what he'd have done to you if I wasn't here. Best get yourself along home, there's going to be trouble in town tonight."

Carl looked scared and puzzled. Ellen watched dumb-founded as Mavis's dad pushed him out the door and onto the street. He didn't even struggle to get free, Ellen thought. I wonder if he has any idea what Mavis's dad is talking about.

She was sure he knew nothing about Peter's medal being stolen. It had to be her grandfather's medal in his hand — why would he have wanted to give her Peter's medal? But what was she going to do? One thing was certain: there was no way she was going home. She had to go to that meeting. She had to find out what was going to happen to Carl.

18

The town hall was packed. Ellen saw Bobby standing near the entrance and hurried over to him.

"Have they started on the bus licences yet?" she asked, looking anxiously around for her mother.

"No, not yet. You probably shouldn't be here, Ellen," Bobby said. "That crowd by the stage have been drinking, and they're in an ugly mood. I'm only staying meself 'cause after the bus thing they're passing a motion to take down the Christmas tree."

"I think I'll just stay for a bit," she said and moved half-way down the hall to stand behind a large potted plant. From there she could see most of the room but could duck behind the plant if she didn't want to be seen.

She looked toward the stage. To the right she saw her dad and Len talking with a small group of men. Ellen noticed some aluminium buckets with stones in them along the wall, close to them. Surely they won't start throwing stones at Geordie? she thought, remembering what Bobby had said about the men wanting to throw stones at the buses.

The mayor and some of the councillors were sitting at a large table on the stage, facing the crowd, but there was no sign of either Carl or Mr. Ramsbottom. Where were they? Did they go to the police station first? Would the police let Mr. Ramsbottom bring Carl to the meeting?

Then she spotted her mam, sitting in the second row from the front. She had her uniform and cap. She had turned around and was talking to Sally Lumsden in the row behind her. Sally was able to get around now, but hadn't been well enough to go back to work yet.

Suddenly Ellen gasped as she spotted Mr. Ramsbottom and Carl standing in the wings of the stage off to her right. Carl looked very frightened. He seemed to be trying to free himself from Mr. Ramsbottom, who had a firm grip on his arm.

A bell rang and the crowd grew quieter. Geordie Cruikshank

and a short, dark-haired man in a navy blue suit, whom Ellen supposed was the man from Newcastle, came onto the stage and sat at the end of the table. Mayor Shuttlewood stood up and spoke into the microphone.

"Next on the list is the application for the bus route from Morpeth to the surrounding area, as indicated on the map behind me." He pointed to a map on the wall. "There are two applicants. First we will hear from Mr. Hemingway, who represents the Unity Bus Company from Newcastle."

"Wait. I have something to say," Mavis's dad came shouting onto the stage dragging Carl with him.

"Order, order," the Mayor banged his gavel. "No comments allowed till after the presentations. Please sit down, Councillor Ramsbottom."

"But —"

"No buts. You know the rules." He motioned to some empty chairs at the end of the table. Ellen held her breath as Mavis's dad scowled then went and sat on the edge of one of them, dragging Carl to the one next to him.

"Now. Mr. Hemingway please," the Mayor said.

Mr. Hemingway came to the microphone with a sheaf of notes and proceeded to explain how his company planned to operate the route. He said they were hoping to get some new buses and eventually extend the service to more of the outlying areas.

"Thank you, Mr. Hemingway. Are there any questions?" the mayor asked.

"Yes, what about the POWs?" someone shouted.

"Our company policy is not to use the prisoners in any way. New jobs will be given first to our returning servicemen, who fought so gallantly during the war," Mr. Hemingway replied.

There were shouts of "Hear, hear" and "Bloody right," followed by cheers and applause from the men near the stage. Then someone started booing and the sound was picked up by the conductresses scattered throughout the hall. It grew louder and louder until the whole room vibrated with the sound. Ellen bit her lip as she saw Mavis's dad scowl again and begin to rise to his feet. But he sat back in his chair as the mayor banged his gavel and shouted in the microphone, "Silence please. Mr. Cruikshank — your turn now." Ellen held her breath and waited anxiously as Geordie came to the microphone.

He stammered a bit at first, then started talking about how he'd run the route for years.

"I hope the council will take into consideration that the local passengers are my main concern. My drivers always wait for people running to catch the buses and they often let people off at their front door if they can't walk from the stops," he said.

He pointed out that older folk were always helped on and off, and the conductresses knew most of the school children by name. He ended by saying how much he cared about the town, that he was hoping to be able to afford another bus and that his life would be over if he had to give up the route. When he sat down Ellen felt a lump in her throat, and she saw some people around her wiping their eyes. Now what's going to happen? she wondered. Surely they won't take the route away from Geordie, but Mavis's dad is going to be mad and —

Then Len shouted, interrupting her thoughts: "What are you going to do about the POWs, Geordie?"

"I have to be honest; I've nothing against the POWs," Geordie replied. "They're hard workers and they're people — just like us. Some of them didn't want to fight any more than our boys, and a few want to stay and live here for good now that the war's over. But most would much rather be home with their families than shovelling my snow. They didn't ask to be kept here, and I won't stop using them."

Some of the women cheered loudly, but there was jeering from the men — not only from Len and his pals, but also from some of the men sitting further back in the hall.

The mayor went hastily back to the microphone. "If there's

no further discussion, I think we should put it to a vote."

"Just a minute. I've got something to say." Ellen's heart started beating like a sledgehammer as Mavis's dad stood up and grabbed the microphone.

"These POWs who work for Geordie Cruikshank are not only the enemy, but they're thieves to boot."

"What are you on about, you stupid old beggar?" This from a woman near the front. "The war's over, haven't you heard?" There was a lot of loud laughter.

"I'm aware of that, madam, but tonight, just before the meeting, I caught this German with something he stole from my house. Something that means the world to my son and to me. This!" he held up the medal toward the audience.

"What's this got to do with the bus route?" Ellen recognized Sally's voice.

"This is my son's *medal* — a medal he was given for bravery in the war, for fighting against the enemy. The enemy that Geordie Cruikshank employs at his bus depot. I say give the route to the Unity Bus Company — a company that'll give our local lads some employment and ignore these thieves. That's where my vote's going. And right after the vote, I'm taking this Nazi down to the police station to press charges."

19

The mayor tried to get Mr. Ramsbottom to sit down, but he stubbornly held on to the microphone. "I'm not finished," he yelled. People started shouting and jeering. Carl sat frozen to his seat, looking terrified.

Ellen stared at the medal in Mr. Ramsbottom's hands. Was it her grandfather's? What was it her dad had said about it? Something about the King. What was it? She struggled to think back. George V was king when her grandfather got his medal, and George VI was king now, so *his* image would be on Peter's medal. Then surely Carl could prove it wasn't Peter's, because this medal wouldn't have George VI on it.

But then it hit her — if that happened, how could Carl explain how he'd got her grandfather's medal? He'd have to tell them about the coat she'd given him, and then everyone would know she was the one who'd helped him escape.

Resisting the urge to flee, Ellen moved closer to the stage. Carl stared right at her and shook his head. Was he trying to tell her to say nothing? Was he trying to protect her? She could just turn and walk away. But what would happen to Carl if she did? And what would happen to her if she didn't? He was facing so much hatred, who knows what would happen to him. He wasn't a thief — she was sure of it. It wouldn't be right to let him take the blame for something he didn't do.

"Wait!" Ellen pushed her way up to the stage and clambered up the few steps. Her knees were knocking, but she went right up to Mr. Ramsbottom and asked, "How do you know that's Peter's medal?"

"You again — I told you to go home. You think I don't know my own son's medal?"

"Maybe it's not Peter's. Please, look carefully at it."

"What do you mean?"

"Please, just look. Which king is on the medal?"

"King? What are you talking about?"

"Please, just look." Ellen held her breath as he turned the

medal over. She was taking a big risk. What if it was Peter's medal after all? But Carl had said it was her grandfather's and she believed him. Her mother's words came back to her: "Stand up for what you believe in." She was shaking as she watched Mr. Ramsbottom turn the medal over, his expression slowly changing from anger to disbelief.

"It-it says King George V — but it has to be Peter's medal. If it isn't, then whose is it?"

"That's my grandfather's medal."

"Your grandfather's? Then how did this Nazi get it? Did he steal it from you? And where is Peter's medal?"

Carl was shaking his head again. Ellen bit her lip. These were the questions she'd been dreading. She could just say he must have found it and was returning it, but then how would he have known it was her grandfather's?

Her mother's words flashed into her mind again: "It's not easy telling the truth, but it's always best in the long run." She remembered Miss Blackthorn saying she admired Ellen's mother for standing up for her beliefs. I don't know if helping Carl escape was right or wrong, she thought, but I do know it's not right to let him take the blame for something he didn't do.

She took a deep breath. "He found it in a coat belonging

to my dad. A coat I gave him before the bomb dropped on Beeswing Yard during the war. We were trapped together in the coalhouses. He was giving the medal back to me tonight when you caught him in the clock tower." There — it was out, and strangely she was no longer afraid. They could do what they liked to her. She'd done what she thought was best. She looked at Carl and he smiled at her.

"*You* helped him escape?" Mr. Ramsbottom blustered.

"Shut your gob and let's get on with the voting," one of the conductresses shouted.

"Yes, I think we'd better or we'll be here all night," the mayor agreed. As he reached for the microphone Mavis's dad pushed him aside.

"No, listen to me. Didn't you hear what she said? This girl's just admitted she helped one of the enemy escape. She must be punished. She has to —" All of a sudden pandemonium broke out and angry words echoed around the room.

"Sit down, you stupid man."

"How much is the Unity Bus Company paying you?"

The conductresses waved their placards again and started chanting, "We want Geordie, we want Geordie."

Then people began pushing and shoving. Ellen saw her mam start up the steps to the stage, her leather money bag raised above her head. Ellen cringed. Oh no, not again. Her dad raced to her side, grabbed her arm and tried to stop her but she pushed him aside.

"Quiet! Quiet!" The mayor desperately tried to make himself heard over the din, but no one took any notice.

Mr. Ramsbottom dropped the microphone and grabbed Ellen's arm, hissing, "Nazi sympathizer!" Then Ellen's mam was pushing herself between Ellen and Mr. Ramsbottom.

"Stop it," she shouted, trying to pull Ellen away from him. "Leave my daughter alone!"

One of the other councillors grabbed her arm and dragged her away. More people climbed onto the stage, and all around Ellen people were shouting and pushing each other. Someone knocked over some discarded scenery, and it caught the curtains, bringing them crashing down with it. Ellen saw someone take a swing at Carl and she watched in horror as he fell to the floor, blood pouring from his nose.

Dust and bits of broken wood were flying everywhere and Ellen started shaking as the panicky feeling of being trapped took hold of her. "Stop it!" she yelled, but no one was listening. "Stop it, stop it, stop it!" she screamed.

"Traitor!" someone shouted. "Jerry lover."

"He was only a boy and he saved my life —"

Suddenly something small and hard came flying through the air and hit her in the chest. Someone was throwing stones. She gasped as more came pelting onto the stage. People started pushing and shoving, falling over each other to get away from the flying missiles. Mr. Ramsbottom let go of her in the chaos.

"Ellen!" she heard her mam yell and saw her reaching out, struggling to get to her. Then her mam was caught up by the crowd, lifted off her feet and swept toward the edge of the stage.

"Mam! Mam!" Ellen reached for her mam's outstretched hands, but just as their fingers touched more stones came hurtling onto the stage and a man came crashing between them, arms flailing, knocking her mam off balance. "No!" Terrified, Ellen watched as her mam staggered backwards, teetered on the edge of the platform, then fell head over heels and landed with a thud on the floor below.

"Mam!" she screamed and jumped down after her. Her dad was right behind her, grabbing her arm and shouting, "Don't touch her. Someone get the doctor, quick."

"Are you all right?" Ellen knelt down beside her mother. She was lying with her eyes closed, her face as white as chalk. She was moaning with pain and her hands were clasped around her stomach. The baby — she's going to lose the baby.

Ellen felt the sour taste of bile in the back of her throat.

The crowd stood watching, shocked into silence. Then someone shouted, "Stand back, give the lass some air."

"Mam, Mam! Speak to me. I'm sorry. I wanted to tell you about Carl but I couldn't. I —"

Ellen's mam opened her eyes and gave her a weak smile.

"It's all right, pet," she said faintly. "Don't you worry."

"Leave your mam be, our Ellen," her dad said, coming up behind her and yanking her to her feet. "Can't you see she's hurt?"

Someone came running in to say the doctor was out on call and it was snowing so hard they'd better not waste any time getting Ellen's mam to the hospital. Before Ellen knew what was happening her mam was lifted onto a makeshift stretcher and hustled out of the room. Her dad followed them.

"Dad —" Ellen ran after them.

"Go on home, Ellen."

"But, Dad —"

"Do as you're told. You've done enough damage for one night."

Stung by the sharpness of his voice, Ellen turned away. She noticed several people in the crowd giving her dirty looks.

"Wait a minute. Best not go by yourself with this lot and

the mood they're in. Get Sally to take you home," her dad said.

"I'll take her." Ellen turned to see Bobby standing behind her. Her dad nodded and Bobby took her hand as they left the hall.

Outside, the wind was howling like a banshee and the snow had swirled into huge puffy drifts. As they battled their way up Newgate Street, Ellen was too numb with cold to think. Bobby didn't say anything, but he held her hand all the way home. As he left her at the door of her flat, she was surprised to hear him mumble, "Good for you." Then, before she could say anything, he turned and headed back up the yard.

It wasn't till she'd climbed the stairs, had lit the fire and was sitting staring into the flames, that she realized what had happened, and what she'd done.

No one would ever speak to her again. Geordie Cruikshank was going to lose his bus licence. And hadn't her dad said that if there was trouble neither him nor her mam would ever get jobs again? And what if her mam lost the baby? The baby!

Suddenly remembering the tiny garment she'd ripped apart, she reached under the chair and pulled out the heap of crinkled wool. She wasn't very good at knitting, but she was going to try. Please God, she prayed as she cast on the stitches, let my mam be all right. I know she's not like my friends' mams, but I wouldn't swap her for all the tea in China. If anything happens to her I'll just die.

She was up to the armhole on the back of the jacket when she heard her dad open the door downstairs. It was almost one o'clock in the morning. She shoved the knitting back under the chair.

"Where's Mam? Is she all right?" she asked.

"They're keeping her in the hospital for a bit. Her arm is broken. She's going to be all right, but they want to watch her." There were dark circles under his eyes. As he flopped down on the chesterfield opposite her, he looked done in.

"And the baby, is she still going to have the baby?" Perhaps she shouldn't have asked. He hadn't wanted to talk about the baby last night.

"The baby's going to be fine."

"When will it — when will it be here?" she asked.

"Early summer, I reckon."

"Oh, I'm so glad." And she was, too. She hadn't wanted a baby brother or sister, but now she realized she'd sort of got used to the idea that it was coming. They sat, uneasy, not saying anything for a minute or two. Then Ellen couldn't stand it any longer.

"I'm sorry I didn't tell you about Carl — about the German," she blurted out.

"Come here, lass," Her dad patted the chesterfield and Ellen moved over and sat beside him.

"That's better." He put his arm around her shoulders. "Now, tell me all about it." And she did. She told him about finding Carl hiding in the coalhouses, about him threatening to kill Squibs if she didn't bring him a coat and about him coming back to save her just before the bomb fell. She explained how he'd helped her get through the awful hours while they waited to be rescued and how they'd become friends.

"Later, after the Home Guard got me out, I went back and let him out. He went off in Sally's boat. He wasn't much older than me, Dad. I just couldn't bear to see him hunted down by Mr. Ramsbottom and those men in the Home Guard." She felt tears running down her cheeks. It felt so good to be able to talk about it at last.

"That was a lot for you to keep to yourself, pet."

"What'll they do to me, Dad?"

"Nowt if I have any say in the matter. You're just a child. Your mam and I wondered what had happened. We had a long talk in the hospital. Your mam thinks you were very brave to face up to Mr. Ramsbottom and tell him the truth, and

I agree with her." Ellen couldn't believe what she was hearing. They weren't mad with her — after all the trouble she'd caused them.

"You know, you're a lot like your mam — going against what people think and getting into trouble for doing what you believe is right. Not that I believe it was right to help a German escape, mind you, but I understand why you did it."

"There's lots that don't think that way, Dad." But if her mam and dad were going to stand by her it wouldn't be so bad facing up to the others, would it? "People are going to be mad at me. Just like they are with Geordie. Oh, what's going to happen to him?" Ellen asked.

"Well, Len stopped by the hospital and said that the mayor had called a quick vote and Geordie gets to keep the route. Then Mr. Ramsbottom resigned from the council. So when your mam's arm gets better she's still got a job — for the time being."

"But what about you? You said if there was trouble nobody would ever give you a job again. And what'll Len do? He wanted the man from Newcastle to get the bus route, didn't he?"

"Aye, he did. But I don't think Len or anybody else is going to be worried too much about buses or jobs for the next day or two. It's still snowing like blazes out there, and I heard on the wireless at the hospital that most of the main roads in the country are blocked. There'll be no buses moving tomorrow, and if we're cut off for long we'll have more to do than fight over jobs."

There'll be no school tomorrow either, then, Ellen thought a few minutes later as she climbed into bed. She was relieved that she wouldn't have to face everybody, yet in a way she wanted it over and done with.

20

Ellen's dad had been right about the snow. For the next two weeks the whole country came to a standstill. There were no buses or cars on the roads. Water pipes froze and burst. Homes were without electricity, and schools and shops were closed. Food supplies fell dangerously low. Outlying villages had to have food airlifted in. Cattle and sheep, out in the fields, smothered in the snow or froze to death by the hundreds. The government declared a state of emergency.

The people of Morpeth had to forget their differences for the time being. Men and women worked side by side, and the prisoners worked with them. Food was shared and canteens set up to feed those who'd run out. People even cracked jokes as they shovelled snow day after day. In the evenings they huddled together in each other's houses to save coal and to keep warm.

"There's nothing like a disaster to pull people together," Ellen's mam said.

Ellen was at the table working on her composition about the suffragettes. Her mam was packing up a basket of sandwiches she'd made for Ellen's dad, Len and two of the POWs. They were out working together to get one of Geordie's buses out of a ditch where it was stuck in two feet of snow.

"It's a bit like the suffragettes, isn't it?" Ellen asked. "When the war started, men and women stopped fighting and pulled together. Then after the war the women were given the vote. I wonder what'll happen here when the snow's all gone."

"I wonder, too. It's not easy to go against someone you've worked alongside during times of trouble. You start seeing things from their point of view."

Like me and Carl, Ellen thought. She'd gone to see him at the hospital. He'd suffered a concussion and his nose had been broken in the fight. He'd apologized in his broken English for "the getting of her in so much trouble."

"But if you hadn't been there with me when the bomb fell

I'd have died. And I never got to thank you for saving Squibs, the rabbit. He lived another year, you know."

"I'm glad. I never really would have killed him."

"I know that now. But how come you ended up back in Morpeth after you escaped in Sally's boat?"

"Sally's boat?"

"The boat you used to get away from the Home Guard. Did you get very far?"

"*Nein*, only to Newcastle. There I was caught and with other prisoners sent to work on a farm. Then I was moved here to Morpeth. I was pleased. Then I could have the opportunity to give back to you the medal."

They talked a bit about their lives. Carl was being sent home soon, and he was looking forward to finally seeing his family again. Ellen told him about the baby, and how much she was looking forward to it.

He and Ellen had exchanged addresses and promised to write to each other. Then she'd bent and kissed him on the cheek, right there in front of everyone in the hospital ward. And she had walked away with her head held high.

She was still worried about facing everyone at school. It wasn't going to be easy and she wondered if they would see things from her point of view. The important ones would, she knew. Mavis had been around already to ask Ellen which photograph of herself she should send to Chris in Canada. And she'd brought Peter with her.

"Peter has something to tell you," Mavis had said.

"I took the m-m-medal," he stammered.

"You what?" Ellen wondered what he was talking about.

"M-my medal. I threw it in the dustbin. I didn't deserve it — not for k-k-killing someone."

"Dad was furious at first, but he and Peter are talking more since then," Mavis said. "They even went out to shovel snow together yesterday."

Ellen was happy to hear this, but decided to keep her distance from Mavis's house all the same. She didn't think Mr. Ramsbottom would be so forgiving of her.

Ellen had bumped into Bobby one day. She'd thanked him for walking home with her after the fight at the town hall. He'd blushed as he said, "It was nowt." Then he'd told her that the Christmas tree was still up, and the baby doves were almost ready to leave the nest. He said he'd like to show her the pictures he'd taken, and Ellen had said she'd love to see them.

Even the *Morpeth Weekly*, which came out four days late because of the snow, was too full of the weather to say much about the ruckus at the town hall. There had only been one tiny paragraph about it on the back page.

"I'm tired, hinny. Do you think you could take the sandwiches to your dad?"

"Yes. It's a bit brighter out — look, it's stopped snowing." Ellen put on her coat and picked up the basket. As she went down the stairs and out the door she met the postman trudging down the yard. There hadn't been any post for days and he had quite a pile of letters.

"One from Canada. Bet we've got more snow here than they have over there this year," he said as he handed her the letter.

Oh, great, another letter from Shirley. But although Shirley's address was at the top left-hand corner of the letter, it wasn't her handwriting, and the letter was addressed to Ellen's mam and dad. Puzzled, she went back into the flat and handed the letter to her mother.

"What's this?" Her mam tore open the envelope with her good hand. "Oh, for goodness sakes," she exclaimed as she scanned the pages.

"What's the matter? Has something happened to Shirley? Is it bad news?"

"No — it's — I don't believe it." Her mam gasped.

"Don't believe what — what is it?"

"They've offered to sponsor us if we want to go to Canada."

"Who has?"

"Shirley's folks. They say there's lots of work there for anyone willing to do anything. And they say we could stay with them till we find someplace to live. They even have a crib for the baby. But how did they know about the baby? And how did they know your dad was out of work?"

Ellen's mind was racing. Now what had she done? She shouldn't have told Shirley all about their problems. Her mam didn't like having what she called their "dirty linen" aired in public. But her mam was smiling, and suddenly she burst out laughing.

"You told her, didn't you? Well, lass, this time you won't get into trouble for blabbing. Wait till your dad hears about this."

"You'd go then — to Canada?"

"You bet your life I would."

"What about Dad? Would he go?"

"Well, let's go ask him right now. If I know him he'll not say no to any kind of job. Of course, we'll have to apply to the immigration people."

Her mam seemed to have forgotten her tiredness as she struggled into her coat.

"I can't wait to see your dad's face when he reads the letter."

Ellen didn't even feel the cold as she tried to keep up with her mam. Her mind was in a whirl. If they went to Canada she'd never see Mavis or Brenda again. And what about Morpeth? She'd miss Morpeth — and Beeswing Yard — a lot. And it would be scary going to a new school, meeting new people, having to make new friends. But she'd decided she wasn't ever going to be scared again, hadn't she?

As they got near the clock tower a shaft of watery sunlight broke unexpectedly through the clouds. Ellen saw her dad and Len with some of the POWs in the marketplace beside Geordie's bus. Her mam ran ahead of her toward them, waving the letter with her good arm.

As Ellen passed the clock tower she noticed a couple of men were taking down the tattered Christmas tree. The birds must have flown the nest, gone off to a new life, she thought. That's what we'll be doing if we go to Canada — starting a new life. A new life, a new home, a new brother or sister, a new future. Whatever it holds I'm ready for it. And Ellen felt a big grin spread across her face as she ran across the marketplace to where her mam and dad were standing together waiting for her.

About the Author

Jean Booker knows wartime England well — she spent her childhood in that country's north. A popular pastime among the young people there was collecting bits of stray shrapnel after an air raid.

At the age of twelve, Jean had pen pals from all over the world. Ten years later, she decided to meet one of them in Montreal. Then she moved permanently to Canada, living first in Montreal, then Toronto and now Bobcaygeon, Ontario.

Jean has been publishing short stories for over thirty-five years. She has enjoyed leading workshops — especially mystery-writing ones. *Still at War* is her third novel for children and the sequel to *Keeping Secrets,* which was shortlisted for the Geoffrey Bilson Award for Historical Fiction for Young People.